Crime Beat Girl

GERI L. DREILING

DEDICATION

For my husband, Enrique.

For my children, Ryan and Casey.

And for my parents, Gerry and Linda.

CONTENTS

ACKNOWLEDGMENTS

It takes a village to complete a novel.

Thank you to Bryan Quertermous for reading a very early, very rough draft of *Crime Beat Girl*. Your feedback was enormously helpful.

Another round of thanks goes to Christine LePorte for content editing and proofreading. Your catches and clean-ups are most appreciated.

A shout-out to my daughter, Casey, the model for the cover of *Crime Beat Girl*. I'll never forget our Saturday morning photo shoot on the lonely streets of St. Louis in the midst of a pandemic.

And most of all, a special heartfelt thank you to my husband, Enrique Serrano Valle. His encouragement and support are vital to my writing. He's always willing to read yet another draft and provide a bit more feedback to help hone my work. And when it comes to creating a cover, I rely on his ability as a photographer and designer to distill my story into one final image.

1 HOMECOMING

Debbie Bradley wondered if her faith in her smartphone's map had been misplaced. The streets were nearly deserted. The homes boarded up. Overgrown grass, knee-high weeds, and sun-bleached trash scattered across abandoned lots. The factories that once churned out shoes, Howitzer shells, and even Corvettes were shuttered. Towering churches now had dark, empty holes instead of ornate stained-glass windows.

The only sound, other than her phone's voice assistant, was the wail of an occasional siren from an unseen emergency vehicle.

She'd grown up in St. Louis and had always been warned that there were places where she shouldn't venture alone—even in the light of day. But she'd been away from home for over ten years, save for the obligatory Thanksgiving and Christmas visits, and she wasn't sure how much of the old advice was still relevant.

Then again, Debbie took advice like she took sugar in her coffee: She shunned it.

She'd always been a contrarian, probably because her parents, Cary Bradley and Beth Hughes, were lawyers. Cary and Beth met in law school, fell in love, and built a law firm representing people who'd been discriminated against at work or preyed upon by big corporations. After her dad died of a heart attack while Debbie was in high school, her mom kept the firm going, and it continued to thrive. There was even a small conference room waiting to be converted into Debbie's office.

Only Debbie didn't want it.

Instead, she yearned to help people in a different way. She believed that as a reporter, she could make a difference by exposing corruption and shining a light on injustice. She loved telling the stories of people and places that her readers might never know. She liked getting away from her desk. She liked digging for the truth. She took pleasure in crafting the sentences that would appear in print or on a screen.

And she was addicted to the buzz she felt each time she saw her byline.

Now, suddenly, she was back home. A place that was both familiar and foreign. Well, physically, she was home. Her heart, however, was still in Washington, D.C. Her mind replayed in a continuous loop those last moments in the nation's capital, loading two hand-me-down roller suitcases into her battered Honda Civic as her fiancé, Christian Garza, pleaded one last time for her to reconsider her decision to take a new job and move back to St. Louis.

He didn't understand all the reasons that made her go.

At some point during their seemingly never-ending engagement, they'd gone from soulmates to roommates. Each time Debbie would suggest a wedding date, Christian found a reason to reject it: too close to the presidential election, too soon after the presidential election, too close to midterms. He'd become obsessed with winning journalism awards. The Pulitzer was the prize he most coveted. Christian was wedded to his job, not her.

When Debbie learned her mother had breast cancer, it was the sign she needed to take the job she hadn't been looking for. In fact, it was a position she initially had turned down.

When Sam Hitchens, her college mentor, became the new editor at *River City*, he reached out to her to see if she was ready to return to her roots. Sam was a traditional newspaper guy but staying afloat at a print paper was getting harder and harder. *River City* magazine had a stable base of advertisers and the wealthy pockets of a native St. Louisan who'd made his money in tech and wanted to dabble in the media. Sam had been tasked with beefing up the magazine, adding real journalism that could be served alongside puff pieces about plastic surgery, expensive private schools, and the latest trendy couch pillow. The tech mogul envisioned a publication that could serve as the social conscience for the city's aristocrats and aging debutantes as well as the professionals and executives of the city who were in a position to make changes to help those around them.

Sam had gotten to know Debbie when he spent a semester teaching as an adjunct at Mizzou, part of a leave of absence he was given while working as the investigative team's editor for the *St. Louis Post-Dispatch*. Before he stepped foot on campus, he'd already been impressed with the legal work of Debbie's parents. Once in the classroom, he saw promise in the daughter of the legal duo. Even after he went back to his regular job at the paper, they'd stayed in touch. She'd send him an occasional clip. He'd give her detailed feedback and suggestions for improvement.

Debbie noticed that her phone had gone quiet. Either she was going in the right direction or her app had crashed. Again. She took one hand off the steering wheel and adjusted her glasses as she peered at the small screen. She put the phone back down and tucked a strand of her thick, wavy hair the color of a roasted chestnut shell back into her tight ponytail. *Maybe it's time to turn back*, she thought. But a retreat wouldn't get her to the Teen Alliance interview.

She needed to focus on the assignment. It was easy enough—interviewing the executive director of a nonprofit. Teen Alliance was an organization trying to give kids from families with little means healthy ways to spend their free time. It would be a puff piece, and although light, fluffy, positive stories weren't really her strength, Sam thought it would be a way for Debbie to get into the groove of magazine reporting, as well as help her grow her contact list of local movers and shakers.

The repeated blare of a car horn shook Debbie out of her reverie.

She turned her head toward the sound that pierced the eerie quiet. It was coming from a blue, rust-pocked pickup truck driven by a silver-haired man. The truck was headed toward her, traveling in its lane, and yet the driver was pointing at Debbie and then pointing at his rearview mirror.

Instinctively, Debbie looked into her own rearview. That's when she spotted a red Audi convertible weaving wildly in and out of her lane—and the truck's lane—and was not slowing down.

Debbie lurched her steering wheel abruptly to the right. The oncoming truck veered in the opposite direction, leaving as much room as possible for the erratic luxury car barreling down the roadway and any driver unfortunate enough to be sharing the space.

The out-of-control Audi swerved toward the truck, then sharply careened the opposite way, its front aimed at Debbie's car. Debbie's heart lurched into her throat. The Audi's tires squealed. The nose of the Audi turned sharply once again and clipped the back end of the truck before jumping the curb.

Screams rang out. A crowd of teens who had been gathered outside a tiny market—the sort that sells junk food, liquor, and lottery tickets in places where chain grocery stores refuse to operate—was in the path of the Audi that was no longer being guided by its driver.

Those on the edges of the group scattered like birds after the loud boom of a gunshot, darting out of the car's path. Those who were in the center, the unlucky ones, flew into the air when the car connected with human flesh.

Debbie slammed on her brakes, threw her car into park, and grabbed her phone to dial 911.

The Audi finally came to a stop after the front end and hood smashed through the display window of the market. Customers still clutching red plastic baskets and a worker wearing a green apron stumbled out the front door, dazed and confused.

Debbie jumped out of her car. There were people broken and bleeding on the ground. Some wailed. One teen who had been tossed in the air and then left crumpled in a heap on the earth looked at Debbie with a vacant gaze, blood trickling from the corner of her mouth.

As Debbie ran toward the Audi, rage filled her chest.

She flung open the car's door with all the strength that anger fuels. The driver, slumped over a deployed airbag, moaned. His feet barely reached the pedals, and his tear-streaked cheeks were round with the baby fat he hadn't lost.

He was just a child.

2 WRONG PLACE, RIGHT TIME

"My baby! My baby!"

Detective Daniel Flannery watched as a woman wearing a gray T-shirt, red sweatpants, and tan slippers with a hole on the right big toe ran toward the crime scene. Two male officers grabbed her, but she continued to push, stretching out her arms to embrace a child that she couldn't see.

A teen who Flannery guessed was about fifteen lay on the ground. At the sound of the woman's voice, the girl's trembling hand lifted into the air. The gesture, although slight, was enough to grab the distraught woman's attention. The woman, who Flannery guessed was the mother of the girl on the ground, screamed louder.

The detective surveyed the chaotic scene with cool detachment. When his brain was on and his emotions were off, his penetrating eyes perceived the smallest details. A cop for over two decades, Flannery had a laser focus that was legendary among his fellow officers, especially the younger ones who had spent more time looking at screens than observing the real world.

Flannery could detect the faint mark left by an old body piercing that had closed back up. He'd find the tiniest sliver of a fingernail underneath a couch cushion. But the story told most often about him involved a peace lily leaf. He spotted it under the radiator located in the foyer of a home-turned-crime-scene and filed it away in his memory. As he toured the house, Flannery, an avid gardener, realized that there was no peace lily among the dead homeowner's many plants. Using that information, he was ultimately able to trace the murder back to a floral shop's delivery driver. The driver had been stalking the victim, who was a regular customer of the business.

Flannery watched as Officer Toni Parker strode over to the wailing mom. Parker was easy to pick out. Her red hair, even when pulled back tightly into a bun, set her apart from the other grim-faced officers with severe buzz cuts. Even without seeing her face, Flannery knew that her lips would be pursed, and when combined with her pointed chin, Parker's young face would take the shape of a sober heart.

He'd known Parker since she was a rookie. With a knack for calming distressed people, she could also summon the tone of a strict mother, one that stopped young criminals for just a moment, their Pavlovian response to their mommas kicking in. Parker was also a symbol of the changes he'd seen in the St. Louis Metropolitan Police Department over the course of twenty years. Staffed with more than 1,300 officers, the SLMPD was no longer the province of the male descendants of Irish, German, and Italian immigrants. Now, it was nearly a third African-American, and women made up more than fifteen percent of the force. And in a nod to the fact that St. Louis was home to the largest group of Bosnians outside of Europe, Slavic language speakers were increasingly being recruited.

Parker gently pulled the woman from the officers. She wrapped one arm around the mother and leaned in close, saying something that Flannery couldn't hear. But he saw the impact of the words. The woman stopped fighting the people who were trying to help.

That's when Flannery noticed a slender woman with glasses and long brown hair swept back into a disheveled ponytail scribbling in a notebook as she sat quietly next to a blanket that partially covered a face, torso, and most of the legs of a body. Only the corpse's feet were exposed. One foot was naked. On the other, a black flip-flop. The toenails, Flannery noted, were painted bright green.

"Shit!" he cursed. The trim detective, in his mid-forties with a square jaw, dark hair, and shoulders so broad that each side could hold a dinner plate, puffed out his chest and struck his most intimidating pose.

"Hey! You!" he said as he straightened his spine to maximize the height that had earned him the tall-drink-of-water nickname from his grandmother.

The young woman bounced. She'd been lost in her thoughts and her notes. For a moment, she was silent, but then, as if waking from a dream, she stood up, blood visible on her navy-blue-and-white-striped button-down shirt. Red streaks marred the cuffs of her tan pants.

"You are?" Flannery asked gruffly.

"Debbie Bradley."

"Well, Miss Bradley," Flannery began.

"Ms. Bradley," Debbie corrected.

"Mzzzz Bradley," Flannery sneered. "What are you doing?"

"I was on my way to Teen Alliance, to interview the executive director for a story I'm working on," Debbie began.

"What outfit are you with?" Flannery asked. "You don't look like a TV reporter."

"Meaning what exactly?" Debbie snapped, taking his quip as a backhanded comment about her appearance not being up to snuff for the screen.

"I don't see a camera crew," Flannery answered, his lips curved slightly, betraying his joy at landing the insult.

Debbie pursed her lips. "I just started at *River City* magazine. This was going to be my first piece."

"New to town?" Flannery fished.

"Back," Debbie responded.

"I'm in charge here," Flannery said. "One of the officers will take down your statement."

"And what will happen to him?" Debbie pointed to a stretcher that cradled the Audi driver, a boy with a bloody face and neck brace whose head was sandwiched between two red blocks to keep his body from twisting.

Flannery answered. "He'll go to the hospital. After that, probably juvenile detention."

"He's just a child," Debbie said, shaking her head. "What's his name?"

"He's a juvenile. I can't tell you that."

Undeterred, she asked, "Where did he get the car from?"

Flannery shrugged. "We'll know soon enough. Now," he said as he waved to Officer Parker, who had just finished guiding the distraught mother into an ambulance, "this officer is going to take your statement."

Flannery turned to Parker. "This is Debbie Bradley, she's a witness. And," he paused, "a reporter.

Take her statement, get her contact information, and then get her outta here."

"Got it," the officer answered before adding, "Ace Towing is on the way to pick up the Audi."

"Jesus, what the hell happened to you?" Sam Hitchens asked when Debbie walked into his office.

Debbie dropped into one of the chairs across from her editor's desk. "I don't even know where to begin."

"Careful of the chairs," he said. "This is a posh place with nice stuff, nothing like a daily newsroom."

Debbie flipped through her reporter's notebook and summed up the afternoon's events, ending with her call to Teen Alliance canceling the interview. The executive director had been understanding. Some of the kids the agency worked with were involved in the accident, so a magazine interview was the last thing on the director's mind.

Sam listened to Debbie's entire tale before opening his mouth. He'd learned long ago it was best not to interrupt reporters coming down from an adrenaline rush.

"Huh, Flannery you say? That guy hates us." Sam shook his head. "I've tried for years to get him to leak bits of information. You know, most cops love the attention of the media even when they pretend to loathe journalists; never met a group of people with more scores to settle, more grudges to avenge. They're often happy to participate in some sort of anonymous whisper campaign while appearing above the fray. But that Flannery, I tell you, he knows everything that's going on, yet he'll never talk—even on deep background. He's an odd one."

Sam paused for a moment, leaned forward, then asked, "Did you get any pictures?"

Debbie pulled out her smartphone and handed the device to her boss.

Sam scrolled through the images, nodding every now and then, before handing the phone back.

Debbie took a breath and made her pitch. "I could write a story about the accident. It could be a first-person essay. A homecoming to one of the nation's most dangerous cities."

Sam sat back in his chair. "There are going to be charges. You'll be a witness. Don't you think it'll be complicated to write a story?"

"Look, if I was a TV reporter who just happened to catch the accident on tape while doing a live feed from the area, there'd be no hesitation about airing the footage. Hell, if I had been livestreaming from the spot with social media and the crash happened, it would be all over the internet."

"I don't know. Some of the media in town may take exception. We write about stories, we aren't the story."

"As long as I disclose that I was a witness, and so long as I stick to what I saw, I don't see a problem. Did any of the reporters who experienced 9/11 stop reporting as they also became part of the story? And there are plenty of magazine narrative nonfiction pieces where the writer is part of the action."

Sam tapped his pen three times on his desk, processing his thoughts before sharing them with his new staffer.

"All right. We'll use your photos—but this is a society pub. So nuthin' too graphic. No blood. No guts. Otherwise, our advertisers and subscribers will go nuts. I want just enough to have people staring and sharing, but I don't want them to feel guilty about being voyeur. We can use this to introduce you to our readers. We'll position you as our fearless new writer."

Debbie rolled her eyes.

"I've been wanting to leverage our online space more. We'll put this on our website, a short story, good pictures, and pair it with a social media push to distribute the content to a wider audience. Hell, we can even do a short video with you. I've been dreaming of going bigger than just print. And our tech overlord wants to see it happen. He's already pushing podcasts. My direction is to make our virtual space just as important as the magazine racks at grocery store checkout stands. I'm an old journalist looking for new ways to do things."

Sam reached for his Rolodex.

Debbie cocked an eyebrow. "Are you sure about looking for new ways of doing things?"

"Hey, I like looking forward. But that doesn't mean I'm willing to throw out what has worked in the past. I've spent years building this personalized database. I don't want to start over. And when was the last time a Rolodex was hacked by the Russians?"

"I have a hard time believing that the Russians would be interested in St. Louis," Debbie said. "Do you also have some carbon paper in your desk drawers?"

Sam scribbled a phone number on a piece of paper. Without looking up, he said, "You got me confused with lawyers in small claims court. You do know that they're still using carbon paper down there, don't you?"

He handed the slip to Debbie. "Here's the phone number for Jill Loomis, the public information officer for the SLMPD. Give her a call to get more details about what happened. You should also take the time to introduce yourself. Make nice. Be charming, if you can manage it. Make new friends."

Debbie frowned. "I still want to wrap up the interview with the Teen Alliance executive director. I hate leaving anything unfinished. And it will give me a chance to cultivate sources."

"Suit yourself," Sam said. "But just make sure that you're on top of the crime beat. It is the start of summer. This is St. Louis. We're in for a long, hot, violent ride. Maybe we can turn your work into an online diary, *Debbie's Diary.* Or maybe," he paused, flashing first true grin that betrayed his amusement, "we'll call it *Crime Beat Girl.*"

"Girl? Really?" Debbie shook her head. "That's very condescending. It doesn't fit my feminist point of view."

Sam shrugged. "I bet you have no problem following *Grammar Girl.* And hey, if 'girl' gets people to check us out each day, eyeballs on the screen, clicks on ads, and new subscribers to daily emails with embedded ads, then I say we try it. And if it works to build an audience, but you still hate it, we'll change it. Okay?"

The reporter sighed as she shoved her notebook back into her purse. "Fine."

Debbie pulled a comb through her wet hair as she walked into her mother's living room.

"What'd you do with your clothes?" Beth asked, looking up from her tablet. She'd been reviewing deposition testimony, highlighting passages in yellow on her screen to prepare for an upcoming trial. She'd ditched paper depositions a few years before, finding that it took less time to compile her notes if she used one of the tablet apps that were being pushed out to lawyers.

Debbie sat down on the impeccably clean cream-colored love seat across from her mother. "I know I could probably get the blood stains out. But I don't want to wear them again; gives me the creeps, so I threw them in the dumpster. Even though that means that my sad selection of clothes is even more pathetic."

Beth nodded, agreeing with her daughter's wardrobe description. The suitcases Debbie had brought back to St. Louis contained more pajama bottoms and workout clothes than professional attire. And even though the mother and daughter were close to each other in size, they were far apart in taste. Debbie wouldn't be caught dead in a navy suit, silk blouse, or tailored pants. *Mom clothes* was how Debbie described Beth's courthouse-and-clients uniforms when she turned down her mother's initial offer to share her closet until Debbie could get on her feet.

"We'll go to the mall tomorrow, after my doctor's appointment," Beth volunteered.

Debbie shook her head. "You're not going to be in the mood to shop after the breast surgeon pokes and prods you. And you've got to meet with the plastic surgeon. Throw in worries about your clients, and you're going to be crabby and uptight."

Beth took a deep breath, fighting the urge to treat her adult daughter like a child. It wasn't easy. Ever since Debbie had returned to St. Louis, the two strong-willed women always seemed to clash. Beth had been against Debbie's move home—and the havoc it would play on her daughter's promising career. Beth suspected that Debbie was running away from her problems in D.C. rather than rushing to help in St. Louis. Even though

Beth wasn't thrilled with Debbie's decision to enter journalism, disrupting that promising career to play nurse to mother wasn't what Beth envisioned for her daughter.

And, as a personal injury lawyer, Beth was more comfortable acting as the champion for others who were hurting. She wasn't accustomed to others helping her. When Beth called her daughter to tell her about the lump in her breast, she never imagined it would trigger a chain of events that would lead to Debbie leaving D.C.—and her fiancé. If she'd known Debbie would make such a fuss, Beth might have kept her cancer a secret.

But now they were back together, struggling to establish new mother-daughter relationship rules.

"Mom, do we have to argue tonight?" Debbie asked softly. "I don't want to fight. Plus, I still need to turn in my final draft to Sam. He's planning on running the story tomorrow on the website."

Beth sighed and pulled her slender, manicured hand through her neatly bobbed hair, dyed a convenient shade of blond that concealed hints of gray. Using a meditation tactic she'd learned to help her cope with the stress of practicing law, Beth envisioned a glass of water inside her stomach. The glass was shaking. Beth took a breath and stilled the water inside the imaginary cup.

"Of course not. I know it has been a long, distressing day for you. Let's start over," Beth began. "Look, I know what your real objection is. You don't like taking money from me. Let's call it a loan. I expect to be paid back once you start receiving your salary. And you know I don't like to shop, so let's make it quick. Browse some clothing store websites tonight. We'll go straight to the clothes you picked out, we'll buy them, and be on our way. Besides, it would be a good way for me transition from the hospital to the office. It is hard to go abruptly from patient asking for medical advice to legal counselor giving advice. An activity in between will help me change my mindset before I go back to the office."

Debbie shrugged. "I guess that makes sense. By the way, I haven't had any time to look for a place to live."

"Why don't you just hold off on that for a while," Beth suggested. "You're still trying to settle into your new job. Focus on that before you take on setting up a new apartment. Besides, my surgery is going to go great. My recovery is going to be quick. You may not be in St. Louis long enough for a one-year lease to make sense. There's plenty of room here in this old house. I will give you your privacy—as long as you give me mine."

Debbie smirked. "You need privacy? For your wild nights reading depositions?"

Beth smiled. "I'm only fifty-six. Believe it or not, life doesn't end after thirty." Beth paused, weighing her words. "I noticed you weren't wearing your engagement ring."

Debbie looked down at her hand. It still felt naked without the diamond on her finger.

"We're taking a break," she answered.

"Hmmm," Beth replied. "Is this mutual, or is it something that Christian wanted?"

Debbie avoided her mother's eyes and muttered, "Mutual."

"You're lying."

Beth knew she was slipping dangerously into the role of a cross-examining lawyer. It was a trait that didn't encourage warm family relationships. Beth took another deep breath and reached for her daughter's hand. "Debbie, I appreciate everything you are doing for me. I am truly grateful. But you don't have to take care of me. I can take care of myself. I don't want you to give up the life you have worked so hard to build."

"Mom, if Christian really loved me, he'd wait. He'd understand why I want to be here now. He'd love me enough to be patient. The fact that he can't do these things makes me wonder if he really did love me. Perhaps he just liked the idea of us—rather than the reality."

"When was the last time you talked to him?" Beth asked.

"A couple of days ago. He called while waiting to review the edits of his story."

Beth turned off her tablet, set it on the coffee table, and got up from the couch.

"My appointment is tomorrow morning at nine a.m. Do you need me to wake you up?"

"Don't worry, Mom," Debbie replied, "I know how to work my alarm and get myself out of bed."

3 GRACE AND SIN

Travis Hunt closed his eyes and lifted his face to the sun, savoring, for just a few seconds, the midday heat caressing his cheeks. His belly, now full of his momma's food—ham hocks, cornbread, and mac and cheese—added to his brief bliss.

Travis had just stepped outside the building that housed his mother's second-floor apartment. Her flat was always dark and cool. She kept the forest-green velvet curtains drawn. That way, she said, it would keep the place from heating up in the humid St. Louis summer; the one air conditioning unit hanging out the living room window wouldn't have to work so hard to keep the sticky air away. But Travis knew his mother had other reasons for the dark curtains. She used them as a shield to keep out nosy neighbors and ne'er-do-wells.

He had stopped at his mom's for a hot shower and some lunch. His mother would open the front door, even though she'd kicked him out several weeks earlier. She'd be happy to see for herself that her nineteen-year-old son was okay.

He knew it had pained her to send him packing, with no place to go except the couches of friends or family who would reluctantly agree to put him up for a few days. But his mother was tired. Tired of having strangers beating on her door at two in the morning looking for garbage that Travis said he knew nothing about.

She was no fool. The folks on her doorstep were always fidgety. They made her nervous. They wouldn't meet her eyes. They avoided looking at the large cross hanging on the wall just inside the front door. Her son would tell the visitors to wait outside. He'd disappear into his room, come back out into the living room with traces of plastic bags sticking out of his sweatshirt pocket. He'd go out into the hallway for a few minutes. Then he'd come back, locking the front door, his back jean pocket stuffed with wrinkled, dirty cash.

When she demanded to know what was going on, he'd shrug: some friends owed him money.

Travis was her oldest child, but not her only one. She had babies that she was determined to save from the streets. She might have let Travis slip away, but she wasn't about to let the others follow in their big brother's footsteps. It was her pastor who told her she had to be like the God of the Old Testament. The most loving thing she could do for them all was to be tough. Travis had to go. Maybe wandering the streets, as the Jews did in the desert during the time of Moses, he would find his way back to goodness. Making him leave was the best chance for them all to find salvation, the pastor had said.

But her resolve had limits. And so, if he needed a meal or a place to wash up, Travis could count on her to open the door—just one more time. And when he left her place, he knew she'd look at him sadly and say, yet again, "I'm praying for you."

And this time it was no different. As he was getting ready to leave, his mother asked him to come to church with her on Sunday. After his vague promise to think about it, she handed him a brown paper bag with three fried bologna sandwiches on white bread slathered in mayo. She'd made them while he was showering. Inside the bag, she stuffed a twenty-dollar bill—a little something to take care of the bus fare that could bring him to church, and maybe back for another home-cooked meal.

Now, standing outside, he tightened his hand around the bag his mom had given him. Even as he felt her love, he also knew the twenty would be gone well before Sunday. He'd never make it to church. But at least he'd left his mom with a shred of hope.

She deserved that.

Before Travis could take another step, he heard the roar of a muffler. A white Malibu was speeding toward him. The tinted windows were rolled halfway down. The barrels of handguns were hanging out of the car and pointed at him.

He didn't need to see who the punks were in the Malibu. He knew they were coming for him.

Travis dropped the bag and turned back to the safety of his mother's. Flinging open the wooden front door with chipped and fading green paint, he tried to make it into the red-brick building that had seen better days.

A shot rang out, followed by several more in rapid succession, sending splinters of green into the air, the sounds of bullets ricocheting off the old tiles. Blood pooled under the gray marble after his body dropped at the base of the stairs.

Debbie thought a lot about Sam's crime beat girl pitch as she sat in the doctor's waiting room with her mom. Beth read court pleadings on her tablet as a distraction from the pending consultation about her upcoming mastectomy. Debbie pondered her place at *River City*.

She still wasn't thrilled about the name, but it was an opportunity. Even though the daily newspaper had a bigger staff, Sam was right about leveraging all the channels of media available to them.

She'd decided to embrace the opportunity. And then she decided to look online for tech tools to help her track St. Louis crime.

She discovered that she couldn't listen to a police scanner. In 2014, the SLMPD encrypted their transmissions so that the public could no longer eavesdrop. After Michael Brown was shot in Ferguson, protesters used scanners to monitor police movements. The cops put an end to the practice when they discovered that the protesters always seemed to be one step ahead.

However, there were alternatives. After a few clicks, she came across a story about an app created by a St. Louis resident. It sent an alert when an emergency call came into the SLMPD. The user plugged in an address and the app would send an email or text with lookout alerts for incidents nearby.

Her search also turned up the SLMPD's Daily Crimes and Happenings report. Each day, the police department posted a summary of crime reports. It listed the date, an address with the last two numbers replaced with XX, and the demographic details of the offenders, victims, and witnesses. It also contained a list of the charges sought.

On this report, Debbie found *her* accident, and she recognized herself as a witness: white, female, twenty-eight years old. The suspect was identified as a juvenile, which meant that the record was sealed. He was charged with second-degree murder, robbery, and assault with a deadly weapon. The dead seventeen-year-old victim, Rainaa Mercer, was identified.

Debbie also discovered a workaround to the sealed record. According to the SLMPD's website, witnesses could request a copy of the police report. Debbie guessed the name of the kid behind the wheel would be marked out, but there would be other breadcrumbs to follow.

Thinking it was at least worth a try, she filled out on online request for the document. Then she promptly forgot about the app and her request as her mother met with the surgeon, a renowned female doctor who was doing one more exam, answering another round of questions before the mastectomy. The initial scans suggested the tumor was no more than possibly stage 2. It wasn't spreading fast. The decision was made to skip pre-surgery radiation. After the operation, the medical team would revisit the questions of radiation and chemotherapy.

Debbie didn't plan on visiting a crime scene. She'd meant to spend the afternoon in the office after Beth's appointment and the brief stop at the mall. But shortly after Debbie sat down at her desk, an email arrived at 2:18 p.m. The subject line: *Person Down.*

"What in the hell are you doing here?" Flannery asked as Debbie walked toward the crime scene with her pen already jotting down observations in a notebook. Even though she only had the first two numbers of the address, the email had provided the street name. All she had to do was drive to the right block, then follow the flashing red lights and yellow police tape.

Debbie forced her lips to smile. "Detective Flannery."

Flannery frowned. "Look, I can't have you taking pictures with your cell phone again and then splashing the images all over the internet. Your photos from yesterday are all over Twitter and Facebook."

"You read my story," Debbie replied. "I didn't take you for a *River City* subscriber, or a social media fan."

"I'm not," Flannery answered. "But our public information officer is. And so is our police chief. And mayor. Plus, we're not a backwoods police department. We've got a robust social media monitoring center that follows internet chatter. I got chewed out this morning because of your article. It isn't just because you're a reporter. You're an eyewitness."

"I disclosed in the story that I was part of the story. My editor doesn't have a problem with it."

"Well, we do. You're gonna screw up our case. Posting pictures and writing articles about accidents you're involved in without knowing the complete story of what went down is dangerous. Your story could be full of errors that were made because you didn't have all the facts. The kid's lawyer is going to come at you with all of the bad information you're putting out there and use it to discredit you."

Debbie could feel her ears warming and hear her voice rising. "Which of my facts are wrong? And I hope you're not thinking of trying to stop me from reporting. Because if you are, we are going have one very big problem. I know my constitutional rights—and I won't hesitate to assert them."

Detective Flannery rubbed his temple with one hand. "You got your rights. I got my orders. You've been on the job how long?"

"Two days."

"Well, congratulations. You've managed to piss off the police department and mayor in record time."

Debbie's lips pursed. She wasn't winning friends nor was she influencing people. But when it came to a reporter's rights, and the Constitution, there was no compromise in her world.

"Look," Flannery said as he shifted his weight from his right leg to his left, "I'm not stupid. I know the legal rules. And this is completely off the record, I'm not gonna stick my neck out so far for this department to try and stop you, as long as you color inside the lines. I know what happens if I go out on a limb. The rest of the local media will pummel me, claim I'm interfering with a reporter. I know how that one ends. I've been through this before. My boss will throw me under the bus and call me a rogue cop, even if I'm only following his hinted orders and the mayor's rants."

Detective Flannery waved for Officer Parker to join them. "Parker, make sure this reporter stays on her side of the yellow crime scene tape."

"Yes, Detective," Officer Parker responded as Flannery turned on his heels and walked away from the two women.

Debbie sighed. "What happened here?"

"Flannery will chew my ass out if I talk to you."

"Well, I don't bite," Debbie retorted. "And I won't use your name. I'm new on this beat, I could use a friend on the force. Parker, right? Are you new to the force?"

Officer Parker looked around to see if anyone was standing nearby. "I've been a cop a couple of years."

Parker rubbed the back of her left hand with the thumb of her right hand. "Look, what I know so far is that it is probably a turf war. Drugs. The victim has a long history of drug arrests and a couple of convictions. You won't be able to find the arrests because they're not public record, but you should be able to find out about the convictions, except anything from when he was a juvenile."

"What's his name?"

"Travis Hunt. I'm sure the public information folks will have more details later."

"Any suspects?"

"All we know right now is that there was a white car. You know how it is down here. Everyone knows who did it, but no one wants to be a snitch." Officer Parker looked around and caught Detective Flannery studying them. "The detective is getting suspicious. I should move away."

"One more thing," Debbie asked. "Would you mind texting me when something happens? I won't tell on you. If you're interested, call me at the office, and I'll give you my cell phone number. I'm not going to give it to you right now—or write down your number—because Flannery keeps looking this way."

Parker straightened her back and squared her shoulders. "We'll see."

At least she hadn't said no, Debbie thought as she walked away from the officer and slipped into the midst of the growing crowd. If what Officer Parker said was true—that everyone knew the shooter but didn't want to snitch—maybe they'd be more comfortable confiding in the press.

It was a long shot, but long shots were all Debbie had.

4 OPTIMISTS AND TROLLS

It was one minute before eleven when Debbie arrived for her appointment with the executive director of Teen Alliance.

The previous twenty-four hours had been hectic. Not that Debbie minded. A packed schedule kept her busy. That was a good thing. It stopped her from fixating on her broken engagement and her mom's upcoming surgery.

After leaving the scene of Travis Hunt's murder, Debbie returned to the office, where she drafted a short post for her new column. The piece was only five paragraphs, but that was plenty long for the readers glancing at her story from their phones. She also uploaded a few photos of the crime scene. Next time, she'd be sure to shoot some video with her phone.

She closed her article with a question: To get witnesses to come forward, what needs to change?

Debbie wanted to provoke comments and conversation. After all, the more people talked and argued in the thread below her story, the longer they'd stay on the website. The longer they were on the site, the easier it was for *River City* to woo advertisers seeking eyeballs. And, of course, the more her column was a must-read feature, the greater job security Debbie enjoyed. This was no small concern when working in a shrinking industry.

She also knew that the debate could summon the trolls. They'd already feasted on her piece about the Audi crash. While some comments were measured and thoughtful, addressing the fact that children don't have fully formed brains capable of accurately weighing the consequences of their actions, others, like one user identified as Rule of Law, were more strident.

"Now we're going to hear that the kid is a good boy," Rule of Law began. "This punk needs to be slammed by the iron fist of the law. Try him as an adult. Send the POS to big-boy prison. He'll be an example for the rest of the thugs on the street."

Sam had deleted some posts, using his forum moderator privilege to yank comments that contained words like shitbum and bastard. "We don't want to alienate our core upper crust audience," he explained to Debbie. "They prefer coded language that is meant to insult. The cloak of plausible deniability."

But there was one comment that struck Debbie as odd. It simply asserted, "This was no accident."

Debbie pondered those four words when she got home. It was the first thing she thought about when she woke in the morning. Perhaps there was someone who knew more about the Audi than she or the police did. And so, after her first cup of coffee, she opened her laptop and returned to her article, looking for clues about the commenter. But the post was gone. And she doubted that Sam would have removed it.

Someone had second thoughts about making a public comment, even a vague one.

For the remainder of the morning, Debbie couldn't shake the feeling that she'd missed an opportunity. Even the police report from that accident that she had requested that arrived in her email wasn't enough to help Debbie forget.

But now, as Debbie was being led back to the executive director's office at Teen Alliance, she found her focus returning.

"Miss Bradley, I'm Darlinda Owens," the executive director said as she rose from her desk and stretched out her hand to greet Debbie with a firm handshake.

Darlinda was wearing a smart, robin's egg blue, sleeveless sheath dress—the sort of dress favored by newscasters and fit female politicians. A brightly colored scarf encircled her neck. Her hair was cropped short. As the two women sat down, Darlinda removed a pair of black glasses, revealing her high cheekbones.

"Seems like as soon as I turned forty-five, my eyesight got worse. I simply can't read without them," she said, flashing a warm smile.

Debbie smiled and raised a hand to straighten her own glasses. "Glasses aren't so bad. I just can't get the hang of contacts," Debbie said, then added, "I'm sorry I had to reschedule our interview."

Darlinda shook her head and sighed. "Please, I understand. I know some of the teenagers who were hurt. And I knew Rainaa. I thought I'd go to her graduation, not her funeral that's scheduled for tomorrow."

"Did you know the driver?"

Darlinda paused and gently traced her eyebrow with her index finger. "Are we on the record?"

"Not if you don't want to be," Debbie answered. "I haven't started taking notes. And I haven't pushed play on my tape recorder."

Darlinda studied Debbie, trying to decide whether the reporter could be trusted. Unsure, the executive director decided opted for a gentle test. "Off the record, yes, I know him. He had just started coming here in the afternoons. He's thirteen."

Debbie frowned. "Geez. Can you share his name?"

"We're trying to make a difference in the lives of young people who, quite frankly, don't believe they have much of a life left. They think that their fate has been preordained. They'll die from a bullet or an overdose—or rot in jail—before they turn twenty-five. My job is to convince them that life is just beginning—not ending. We offer hope and provide a path and the guidance they need to find a way out of poverty. This is our mission. And we couldn't do it if our community didn't trust us. That's my long-winded way of saying that no, I can't give you his name."

Debbie nodded. "I understand. And I hope you understand that I wouldn't be doing my job if I didn't ask."

Darlinda nodded. "Now, shall we go on the record?"

Debbie pushed play and picked up her pen and notebook.

The executive director explained that Teen Alliance had spent the last eight years working to help neighborhood children. They focused on teenagers, which they defined as eleven and above.

"If we wait until they're thirteen, we're afraid of losing them to the streets," Darlinda said.

Teen Alliance had converted the first floor of an old public school into a safe space. The Saint Louis Public Schools allowed Teen Alliance to use the space rent-free—but the nonprofit had to pay for utilities and maintenance on the first floor. Kids could play basketball or ping-pong, use the computers, talk to a counselor, and socialize in a supervised environment where drugs, guns, and violence were forbidden if you wanted to walk through the organization's doors.

"Come with me," Darlinda said as she rose again from her desk. "I'd like to give you a tour, so you can see what we do. And even better, I'd like you to meet some of our teens."

As the two women began their walk through the facility, Darlinda explained, "The gift from the city is wonderful—but there are financial burdens that come from the agreement. This school was built in the 1920s. Like anything that's a century old, it has maintenance issues—even if we don't have to cover the really big-ticket items like the roof and the boiler."

The pair walked into a classroom. An air conditioning window unit blasted cold into the warm, cavernous space. Yellow paint and murals of St. Louis scenes such as the Mississippi River and landmark churches in North St. Louis covered the walls. Inserted into the art were teens reading books and wearing graduation caps. In one corner of the room, bean bags were arranged around a large rug. Three teenagers lounged in the area, passing a phone among themselves, laughing as a video played.

In another corner was a row of desktop computers. In front of a screen sat a young man, his fingers flying across a keyboard.

"We've made some strong connections with many area businesses," Darlinda said. "Sometimes, we receive donations like these computers which are a real help. Sometimes, and this is off-the-record, we receive gifts that miss the mark just a bit such as GPS bike trackers."

The boy who'd been sitting at the computer jumped in without looking up from the screen. "Yeah, no one 'round here would go out and ride a bike. That's how you get mugged. Or worse."

"Jarrett," Darlinda said to the boy, "I'd like you to meet Debbie Bradley, she's a magazine writer."

The keyboard went silent and the teen finally looked up. "Hi," he said politely.

Darlinda explained. "Jarrett Compton started coming to Teen Alliance after we first opened. Now, he's seventeen and about ready to start his senior year of high school. Perhaps you can tell that Jarrett likes computers."

The young man's eyes widened at the word computers.

Debbie smiled at the boy. "What do you like about them?" she asked.

"Everything! I got hooked on video games when I was young. But now that I'm older, I know that I don't want to just play video games, I want to code them."

Darlinda added, "We've taken Jarrett on tours of the two tech startup hubs in St. Louis, including one of the hubs that is being underwritten by *River City*'s publisher."

"What'd you think?" Debbie asked, knowing open-ended questions usually yielded better quotes.

"Wow!" was all Jarrett said.

Darlinda picked up where Jarrett stopped. "We're working to find him a mentor. Plus, we're in regular contact with Jarrett's school counselor. He needs a college with a strong software engineering program, one that will help him with the tuition. We're also going to introduce Jarrett at our charity event this weekend."

Darlinda paused for a moment. "Debbie, you should come. We have an influential board of directors, including the mayor. They make our work possible. And maybe it would be a chance for you to make some connections."

Man, you're good, Debbie thought to herself, admiring Darlinda's shrewd use of influence.

"Sure, that would be great," Debbie said. "Would you mind if we took some pictures of Jarrett that night and shared his story as one of your successes?"

Darlinda looked at Jarrett. "It's up to you. And your parents."

Jarrett smiled broadly. "I don't think it is going to be a problem. And my granny will be all excited to tell her friends at church."

Upscale suburban neighborhoods all looked the same to Debbie. The same mailboxes, the same garages, the same four architectural styles: white columns, light-colored brick ranch homes, faux Bavarian lodges, or red-brick two-stories. They were plopped down on maze-like streets with names like Deer Road, Deer Court, Deer Avenue, Deer Springs, Deer Ranch, and Deer Acres.

Debbie was biased against the suburbs. She knew it.

She had grown up in the city. Her parents had chosen to live in a house built in the late 1800s, one splashed with bright Victorian colors of light blue and window trim painted a purple-blue. Yet her classmates, the ones who attended an elite, private all-girls' high school with Debbie, lived in the suburbs with zip codes favored by the well-to-do. Those parents feared the city, unless it was to drive downtown for a baseball game. They wouldn't let their daughters spend the night at Debbie's house. As a result, Debbie became a reverse snob despite Beth and Cary's best efforts to encourage their daughter to think of herself as an ambassador for the city.

Instead, Debbie was annoyed by the ignorance, stereotypes, classicism, and racism. She didn't feel patience, nor did she feel compassion. Even now, after a long absence, she had slipped back into her biases.

She was in the area hoping to interview the owner of the red Audi, Hank Frederich. She'd uncovered the nugget of information about the car's owner in the police report she'd received that morning in her email, the one she had requested while waiting for her mother's doctor's appointment.

Debbie glanced at her phone. It was just after 6 p.m. as she walked up the driveway and rang the doorbell. Hopefully, the owner was home from work.

The door opened. "Yes?" asked the middle-aged man with salt-and-pepper hair and a protruding stomach that suggested he was a white-collar office worker. Of course, the now-crashed Audi also hinted at some sort of decent-paying office job, or a good-enough trust fund.

Debbie introduced herself, her voice lilting higher at the second syllable of her last name. The inflection didn't come naturally to her because her parents trained her to speak like a competent lawyer, not like a girly-girl. But she'd noticed that uptalk encouraged people, particularly men, to drop their guard. Turning statements into slight questions using a higher pitch in her voice made her more feminine, less threatening.

"I'd like to ask you some questions about your car. The one that was stolen?" Debbie said, once again making the last statement sound more like a question.

The man pursed his lips. "What? Are you with an insurance company? Or with that lawyer's office, what was his name, Chase Laclede?"

Debbie, widening her eyes innocently, said with a smile. "No, I'm a reporter."

"Look, I don't have anything to say to a reporter," Hank said as he started to close the door.

Debbie knew she had to act fast if she was going to get any information. She'd perfected the art of just one more question, a stalling tactic that could keep an unwilling interviewee talking just a little bit longer, and now it was time to use it.

"Please, I just wanted to know where your car was stolen from," Debbie asked innocently. The please was also calculated. People tended to respond better when you started with please.

"Downtown. I was downtown for a baseball game. I went to my car after the game was over, it was no longer there."

"Have you been able to get your car back?" Debbie followed up, breaking her one-more-question promise that she really never intended to keep.

"Naw, but I did get a chance to talk to the cops. They didn't find anything of mine in the car. Not that I'm surprised, I didn't have anything in my car. I know better than to leave things in it. That's just an invitation for a break-in when you go the city."

"Did they tell you who they think stole it?"

"I guess it was that thug who wrecked it," Hank said.

Debbie flinched at the epithet, but the word seemed to loosen tongue of the Audi owner, especially when she didn't object to its use. "His lawyer came by here yesterday asking questions."

"His lawyer?"

"Yeah, I told you when I opened the door. Chase Laclede. Now look, I got nothing to say to you."

The door slammed. Debbie smiled. At least she'd managed to gather just a bit more string that might help her weave a story.

"What do you know about Chase Laclede?" Debbie asked her mom.

The two women were sitting in the kitchen eating the sandwiches that Debbie had picked up after interviewing the Audi owner. It had been a long day for both mother and daughter, and neither was particularly interested in cooking anything.

"A smart young lawyer. Idealistic. And, objectively speaking, he is quite handsome. He has the most beautiful green eyes," Beth said.

"You notice these things?" Debbie asked.

"Of course," Beth scoffed. "You're not the only one who has a job that requires attention to detail. I'm not interested in dating him. He's just a boy. But his father..." she said, shaking her head slowly.

"What about his father?" Debbie asked with a smile.

"I've had some dealings with David Laclede," her mother said. "He's general counsel for one of the big manufacturing companies here. We've been on opposite sides of lawsuits."

Beth took a sip of chamomile tea. "He's difficult. Smart. Extremely difficult. He'll make you fight every little motion, no matter how trivial. He frustrates me to no end. But he has an interesting back story. He grew up here in St. Louis. He lived on the North Side. The son of a single mom who worked as a nursing home aide. He went to public schools then got his degree locally, at University of Missouri-St. Louis. But he was smart, real smart. After working for an insurance company for a few years, he made it into Northwestern Law School and married a law school classmate, Dee, who was from Chicago. It was harder back then to be a biracial couple—he's black, she's white. Even though Dee could've gotten a job with one of the big law firms here in town, she chose to become a public defender. She left the P.D.'s office after Chase was born. From what I understand, even though Dee isn't practicing, she is involved in nonprofit efforts and works tirelessly to raise funds for causes that she believes in. From what I can tell, Chase seems to have found a way to combine the aggressive attributes of his father with his mother's sense of social justice. At least for now."

"Interesting," Debbie said as she lifted the top of her sandwich to inspect the contents inside.

"Why do you ask?"

"He represents the boy who was driving the stolen car. I'd like to interview him—and his client."

"Pffff. Good luck with that. He's interested in trying his case in court, not in the press. He's not going to want to chat with you. And he sure as heck isn't going to let you talk to his client. So don't think that sweet charming act of yours that I've seen you trot out will work on Chase. He may be young, but he's not gonna fall for that fakery."

Debbie split a chocolate chip cookie as big as the teacup saucer and handed half to her mom. "How are you feeling?"

"Fine," Beth answered. "I've got a mountain of work that I need to complete before my surgery. I don't know what I would've done if the doctor had said I needed radiation before my mastectomy."

"Well, it still sucks," Debbie said.

Beth shook her head. "Right now, I've got a shattered family I'm representing. The dad was killed by a semi on the highway. The toddler in the car is in critical condition and may not make it. The mom is trying to plan a funeral with no money, trying to figure out how to pay medical bills with shitty insurance. And she's afraid to leave her baby's bedside. I'm sitting here in my comfortable house with a fat savings account enjoying a cookie with my healthy daughter. No, my dear, my life does not, as you so eloquently put it, suck."

5 ANGELS AND LAWYERS

The younger the deceased, the larger the crowd that gathers to grieve. And this funeral was no exception. As Debbie slipped into a pew near the back of Zion Missionary Baptist Church, she thought about all the funerals she had attended over the course of her career. She could not imagine becoming immune to the sorrow that is the last goodbye to a child's lifeless body.

From her seat, Debbie could see an open white casket lined in pink satin. Rainaa was nestled inside. Next to the casket, an enlarged framed photo of the teen—a smiling picture from some happy occasion—had been placed on a stand.

As the minister got up and began to speak, Debbie pulled out her notebook to try and capture his words and the crowd's reactions. Even though the man of faith's hair was graying at the temples, his body still possessed the vigor of a younger preacher. When the minister opened his mouth, a hypnotic voice flowed through it. His speech was more of a melody; one that pushed and pulled the crowd through a range of emotions.

"Babies!" he cried out. "Hold your babies close. Hold your babies tight. And love your babies every single blessed day. You never know when they will be called back to heaven to rejoin their Almighty Father." He paused. "Their first Father."

An old woman dressed in a perfectly tailored pink suit, her white hair just barely visible underneath a matching pink hat with a bow affixed to the front, sat next to Debbie. The woman shut her eyes as she concentrated on the preacher's words. "Mmmhmmm," she said, responding to the minister. "That's right."

The preacher continued, looking at the girl's parents in the front row. The reverend explained that both parents had been at work on the day the Lord summoned their daughter. Her father was a mechanic who worked at a repair shop near the home. Her mother was a salesperson at a mall department store. When they said goodbye to their daughter at the dawn of the day that would shatter their lives, they had no idea that it was the last time they'd see each other. "But," he promised, "they will be together again—in the next life."

The minister paused. The congregation stilled.

"My brothers and sisters, let's not forget Joshua Lucas," he said softly. "We must keep our children safe, and keep a watchful eye on them, so that they don't become vessels bringing sadness and grief, like Joshua." He shook his head and slammed both hands down on the pulpit. "Evil forces have been unleashed on our streets. Now, brothers and sisters, please remember that we have two children who need our prayers."

Debbie had a lead. She had the boy's name.

"Amen!" said the old woman in pink next to her.

Debbie turned slightly to get a look at the woman who was moved by the pastor's words. That's when she noticed that Jarrett, the young man she'd met at Teen Alliance, was sitting next to the woman. Jarret caught Debbie's glance and gave her a shy wave. He leaned over to the woman in pink and whispered into her ear. She turned to look at Debbie, narrowing her eyes and pursing her lips at the sight of the reporter's notebook.

Then she turned her body slightly away from Debbie, raised her head high, and refocused her attention on the preacher.

Chase Laclede shoved the few documents that had been on his desk into brown legal folders. One could never be too careful with reporters. He'd seen too many lawyers stung by sloppiness and ego. Lawyers happy to get their pictures taken by the media only to have the contents on top of their desks later magnified, exposing confidential information.

It didn't take long to put everything away. Most of his clients' files were now stored in the cloud. But there were still a few paper documents still scattered across his desk, items that the receptionist hadn't yet scanned. She was, after all, rather busy because her labor was split amongst the four attorneys who shared an office space but had separate practices.

"Ms. Bradley, pleased to meet you," Chase said as the receptionist escorted the reporter into his office, extending his hand over his now tidy desk to greet her with a firm shake.

"Thanks for seeing me, Mr. Laclede."

Debbie had written her story about Rainaa's funeral shortly after it was over. It was a heartbreaking piece. And after she sent it to Sam, she knew she needed to get away from her desk. It was late afternoon. Lawyers often made it back to their office near the end of the day, so Debbie decided the best chance she had to talk to Chase was to just show up. Sometimes a surprise ambush worked.

The young lawyer gestured to the guest chair and then sat down behind his desk. "I don't usually meet with people who don't have an appointment. I hope you appreciate the exception that I made for you."

Debbie smiled; perhaps her mother had misjudged Chase Laclede's willingness to talk to her.

Chase continued, "I made the exception because you're a witness in a case I'm handling. You've been on my list of people I need to interview."

Debbie frowned. She hated it when her mom was right. She flipped open her notebook. "I want to interview you, too."

Chase folded his hands together and placed them on the desk. He was quite handsome, Debbie had to admit, even with the dark shadows circling his eyes. The degrees hanging on the wall were impressive: an undergraduate degree from the University of Texas at Austin, a law degree from Washington University in St. Louis. According to the diploma, he'd only been out of school four years, so that made him twenty-nine or thirty. In her mother's words, he was just a baby lawyer.

Chase took a deep breath. "Ms. Bradley."

"Please, call me Debbie."

"Debbie. You can't expect lawyers to discuss their clients with journalists, especially clients who are children."

"I understand," Debbie said in her most agreeable voice. "I can assure you that my magazine's policy—and my own policy—requires me to keep the name of a juvenile charged with a crime confidential. At least until he or she is certified as an adult."

"What about your conflict-of-interest policy? Don't you think it is, um, ethically questionable that you're writing a story where you're also one of the main characters?"

"No. Not in this instance. I've already explored this with my boss. I always take care on each piece to disclose my role as a witness, much like many media companies do when writing about their corporate owners. And immersion journalists haven't shied away from appearing in their work. Gay Talese couldn't have written 'Frank Sinatra Has a Cold' without highlighting Sinatra's efforts to evade an interview. Joan Didion's piece 'John Wayne, A Love Song' includes her recollections of a dreamy dinner with the actor. Hunter S. Thompson wrote about his time with the Hells Angels. And today, of course, you've got online sites like Vice embracing first-person journalism."

"But the difference with those cases is that you are part of a potential court proceeding."

"My experience was extremely limited. I heard the honking. I saw the car in my rearview mirror. I saw the crash. And I found the boy in the front seat. That's it."

Chase leaned forward. "Why don't you elaborate on those experiences?"

Debbie shrugged and recounted in the very same detail the article she'd written about the experience on the first day. It was also the same information she'd shared with Flannery and Parker.

Chase scribbled as she spoke. When she was done, he put his pen down. "That's pretty much what the police report said. Did you take notes at the crime scene?"

"Yes."

"And from what I saw online, it looks like you have pictures. Did you publish them all?"

"No."

"You do realize that I can subpoena your notes and your photos, don't you? The so-called reporter's shield is weak, it snaps like a dry twig when the reporter is a witness. Not that it is much of a protection in the first place."

Debbie pursed her lips. "I'm not gonna give up my notes without a fight. That is a matter you're going to have to take up with *River City*'s lawyers, and our publisher."

Chase frowned. He still hadn't decided whether that side fight would be worth the effort. "Who's to say that your notes won't be subpoenaed by the prosecution? You've created quite the ethical pretzel, Debbie Bradley."

Debbie opened her notebook. "Do you think your client will stand trial as an adult?"

Chase replied, "I'm not going to answer specific questions about this case."

He looked out the window for a moment before continuing. His client needed her as an ally, not an adversary. "Look, I can explain the law in general."

In Missouri, Chase said, a child as young as twelve could be certified to stand trial as an adult. But the state would also need to show factors such as a criminal history or viciousness associated with the crime.

"Okay, that makes sense," Debbie said, also trying to entice Chase into her corner. "You know, my mom is a lawyer here in town," she added, hoping that sharing a piece of personal information would encourage Chase to do the same. "She says she doesn't know you personally, but she swears you've got an excellent reputation. She said you were known as smart, hardworking, and dedicated to your clients."

Chase's eyebrows drew closer together as he studied the reporter who was doing her best to find something in common with him. "Who's your mom?"

"Beth Hughes."

His face lit up. Dropping her mother's name had been like sharing a secret password needed to get into an exclusive club.

"She's a legend in the personal injury legal circles. My dad has grumbled about her during many family dinners. He's annoyed at her skill and dedication. It causes him a lot of problems. Why didn't you follow in your mother's footsteps and become a lawyer? Believe me, I know there had to have been pressure to join the profession."

Debbie shook her head. "Growing up, it always seemed like my parents were stressed out. My father was a lawyer, too."

"Of course," Chase said. "I do remember that Beth Hughes was married to Cary Bradley. Bradley & Hughes, LLC. Your mom kept the firm name. Perhaps she was saving Bradley for you?"

Debbie nodded. "Whenever there was a big trial, there was so much stress at home. I wanted nothing to do with that life."

Chase looked at his watch. "Well, it is after six p.m., and you're here. Sure you're not like your mom?"

Debbie shrugged and smiled.

Chase drew in a deep breath. "I hope I'm not stepping out of bounds, but I heard about your mom's cancer. I'm sorry."

Debbie sighed. "How did you know?"

"You're from St. Louis. You know that this is just a big little town. And when it comes to the legal profession, it is an even smaller, more tightly knit circle. News travels."

Debbie looked away for a moment, caught off-guard by his genuine compassion. "I appreciate that. I'll be sure to let my mom know."

Debbie paused. "You know, it's ironic. I thought the diagnosis would slow her down. Instead, she's even more determined and unstoppable. I don't know if she's worried she won't have enough time to take care of her clients. But I really wish she'd take care of herself."

"Maybe she is taking care of herself. Maybe she just doesn't want to think about it. I know it is easier to focus on the problems of others than to focus on your own problems. Especially when it seems like there isn't much you can do."

Debbie nodded; what he said made sense.

"Hey, you sure are good at switching the subject," Debbie said as she realized he was a master at re-targeting the conversation.

Chase laughed, a genuine and relaxed moment of humor.

"Look," Debbie said, "I'm not going to disclose your client's name. But I am trying to find out how a thirteen-year-old got his hands on an Audi. I doubt he was the one who stole it."

Chase leaned forward and asked, "What makes you say that?"

Debbie referred to the police report instead of revealing she'd talked to the Audi owner. The car had been stolen from downtown. Joshua was a good eight to ten miles from the ballpark when he crashed. He wasn't an experienced driver.

Chase rubbed his chin. "An interesting theory."

Debbie scribbled in her notebook and tore out a piece of paper. Chase might be a formidable adversary, but he wasn't an enemy. "Here's my contact info. In case you need to send me a subpoena, or you want to give me a tip. It doesn't have to be about this case. I'm always looking for stories."

"Paper? No business card?"

"I'm new. And my employer is slow."

Sam's text arrived while she was interviewing Chase. But it was only after she had left his office that Debbie dared to look at her phone because listening, really listening, was hard work, at least for Debbie. During critical interviews, she was unable to focus on the conversation and the pinging of her phone at the same time. The phone could wait. But when it came to difficult and important interviews, she might only get one shot.

Sam's missive began with the good news and bad news approach. The good news? The piece on Rainaa's funeral only required a few grammar tweaks. So Sam had it posted online. The bad news? *River City*'s lawyers were anxious about Debbie's coverage of the accident.

"Shit," Debbie whispered under her breath as she got into her car.

Her first impulse was to call Christian and ask for his advice. Should she stop writing? Was it really questionable for her to publicly tell the world what she'd seen and heard, so long as she also was transparent and explained her role in the accident? Where was the balance between free speech and an accused's right to a fair trial?

Debbie reached for the phone she'd tossed on the passenger's seat. Fighting the urge to call him, she opened her former employer's newspaper app to see if Christian had written anything new. Debbie groaned. The lead story belonged to Christian; the latest revelation of never-ending corruption emanating from the White House and an administration that seemed to delight in self-dealing.

That's when the phone pinging started. A news junkie, Debbie had enabled alerts from several national news outlets. And they all started sending her stories based on Christian's reporting.

"What have I done?" Debbie muttered under her breath. She'd left a national newspaper during a critical moment in American history. Her ex-fiancé's career was on fire. Here she was in flyover country, chasing a kid car thief.

Debbie sighed. She may as well check her office voice mail. When she dialed in, she was surprised. "Ms. Bradley, Toni Parker here. I'm going to give you my personal number. Call me from your cell so I can get your direct line."

Debbie punched the numbers into her phone. Officer Parker didn't pick up, but Debbie left a return message. Now at least they had a connection.

Debbie started her car. The Teen Alliance Gala was tomorrow. Maybe her mom would have a suitable dress she could borrow. Beth was always going to some sort of Legal Aid fundraiser. There had to be something Debbie could wear that was simple, but not too middle-aged-lawyer-lady.

Tonight, maybe she could convince her mom to stop working for a little bit. She would pick up a bottle of wine and maybe they could watch a movie together, maybe *Casablanca*. Debbie would enjoy listening to her mother launch into her argument, once the movie was over, that *Casablanca* should be remade, only this time, the characters of Rick Blaine and Victor Laszlo would be played by women. Ilsa Lund would be a man.

"I'd like to see how the audience would react to two women deciding who the man should be awarded to for the sake of the free world," Debbie knew her mother would mutter before heading off to bed.

6 PRIDE AND PUZZLES

Debbie got out of her car and gave the bottom of the black dress one last sharp tug. She was there for a story, not to draw attention to her shapely legs.

Revealing clothes didn't mesh with work. She preferred to concentrate on reporting, rather than worry about covering her backside. Plus, dresses interfered with getting the perfect picture.

At least the dress didn't fall too far above the knee. It was, after all, her mom's. Debbie hadn't bothered to pack black-tie-affair clothes as she made her quick getaway from D.C. The dress she settled on was the best of the bunch in her mother's closet. *Paupers can't be picky,* she reminded herself. Actually, she had to admit she looked pretty good. And, despite cancer, her mom was in amazing shape.

But even the hope of good genetics wasn't enough to overcome her bad mood. Parking was a nightmare. Most of the attendees were using the pricey valet service. She hadn't received her first paycheck yet so her bank account, like her dress, left little room for miscalculation. And pride prevented Debbie from asking her mother for a few more bucks.

After circling the area around the hotel several times, Debbie squeezed into a snug parking space. The back bumper of her Civic crossed ever so slightly over into the no parking area marked by a yellow line on the curb. An inch, maybe two at the most, she guessed. Not enough to be illegal. It would do for a few hours.

The board of directors for Teen Alliance consisted of the who's who of St. Louis money. Some of the people who sat on the board were the same folks who were fixtures of the debutante ball scene that was an embedded part of St. Louis society. Even as a teen, Debbie found the idea of debutantes ridiculous. Tonight, she would have to play nice with this group for her story, and that was also making her a bit sour.

Debbie was the type of reporter who preferred crime scenes to society soirées. In some ways, Debbie thought, it was easier to be a reporter in a place where you weren't raised. New places meant that old experiences and resentments didn't color your judgment.

Debbie adjusted her shoulders. Her muscles were tight and drawn. She needed to loosen up. She asked herself: *Where is the opportunity?*

The answer was obvious. The gala was also about social justice and good works. If she was just focused on that fact—and Jarrett, the high schooler who had big dreams of college and coding—she could, perhaps, talk herself into a better mood. And a room full of movers and shakers meant cultivating sources—a chance to expand her circle of contacts—the currency that every reporter sought and hoarded.

"Debbie!" It was the executive director of Teen Alliance, Darlinda Owens.

"I'm so glad to see you," Debbie said with relief. "I always feel out of place at these things."

"I'm delighted you could come. Jarrett will be thrilled. He talks about you constantly. He told me that he saw you at the funeral the other day. And whenever I see him, he asks me if I'm reading your work."

Debbie smiled, slightly embarrassed. For someone who loved to ask people questions about their lives and accomplishments, she was always a little hesitant to talk about her work. Maybe she'd received one too many admonishments as a Catholic school girl about the dangers of pride. Debbie switched the subject. "I did see Jarrett. He was sitting next to an older woman."

"That would probably be his grandmother, Ada Davis. She's formidable. Precisely the type of person we seek out within the community to get buy-in for our mission," Darlinda explained. "If we aren't trusted by the family gatekeepers, if we don't have their blessing, we're just another set of do-gooders that outsiders keep at arm's length. Anyway, she is here. As are Jarrett's parents. They're all seated at the head table."

Debbie spotted the grandmother and grandson sitting across the room. Jarrett was wearing a starched white button-down shirt and a red tie. His hand kept traveling up to the neck collar. Debbie empathized with his discomfort. Ada Davis was wearing a neatly pressed jacket and skirt, the color of both as red as a cardinal, with a white collared blouse and a gold pin fastened at the neck. Her back was straight and tall as she sat in the chair. She was beaming with pride even as, Debbie guessed, Ada was gently reminding her grandson to stop tugging at the neck of his dress shirt.

The ornate ballroom of the Chase Park Plaza was immense. Classic chandeliers with warm lights hung from the ceiling. Accent lighting scattered throughout gave the place a romantic glow—perfect for the high-class affair. White tablecloths covered round-top tables arranged with a collection of small yellow and white flowers in the center. On either end of the ballroom, cash bars had been strategically placed. Each seat had cost $200, which Debbie quickly concluded meant that one table was worth $2,000. And there had to be at least 30 tables. Probably more. And that didn't include the silent auction and random generous gifts.

Debbie recognized this place. It was where lawyers often held fundraisers for Legal Services of Eastern Missouri. Her parents had been avid supporters, and they'd taken Debbie along when she was a teen, hoping that exposure to the legal profession would entice her to join their ranks one day.

Their efforts had the opposite effect.

"I didn't know you'd be here," a man said from behind Debbie.

"Chase Laclede! What a pleasant surprise."

"Somehow I didn't imagine that you'd find your way back into St. Louis society so quickly," Chase said.

"I can barely afford to park my car, let alone buy a ticket for the event. I'm writing a story about Teen Alliance. I was on my way to meet with the executive director the day I encountered your client. Darlinda introduced me to Jarrett. She thought he might make a good face for a story."

"Face?" Chase asked.

"Readers relate to people, not organizations or causes. It is one thing to write a general piece about kids growing up in where the odds are most decidedly not in their favor. Or you can write about organizations, like Teen Alliance, and list their various virtuous deeds. But it doesn't really resonate emotionally with the reader. What sticks are stories about real people who have real problems and struggle to overcome the obstacles in their way. It's only through the example of real life that a writer can explain the impact of a policy or a nonprofit's work or even a corporation's wrongdoing."

"I see," Chase said, nodding his head. "A case, a trial, is also a story. And a lawyer tries to humanize the plaintiff or defendant so that the jury can feel some empathy. My dad would say that humanizing a corporation is particularly hard."

Debbie smiled and nodded. "Yes, I can imagine."

"Come with me. There's some people you should meet."

Chase offered the crook of his arm for Debbie to take. A formal gesture that belonged in a different time. For Chase, Debbie guessed, it was probably a vestige of escorting a debutante maid in taffeta or satin at the Veiled Prophet Ball.

Debbie decided to go with it. And when she lightly looped her hand around his arm, she could feel the hint of muscle underneath the tuxedo. Standing this close to him, it was impossible to miss the fresh smell of soap and light splash of aftershave. And she thought of Christian.

Chase led to her a couple close to her mom's age.

"Debbie, I'd like you to meet David and Dee Laclede. Mom and Dad, this is the reporter I was telling you about, Debbie Bradley. She's the daughter of Beth Hughes and Cary Bradley."

David and Chase shared similar builds, although the father's waist was a bit wider. Dee was a petite woman with smile wrinkles around her blue eyes. Her neat dark bob framed her small face.

"I'm pleased to meet you," Debbie said, extending her hand to David and Dee. "A family of lawyers?"

Dee laughed. "Yes, but we use our skills in different ways. We each want to do some good, though how we define good differs."

David Laclede cleared his throat. "Yes, my wife wants to help nonprofits get exposure and raise money. I like to help corporations stay in business and give people jobs so they can support their families. And my son, well, the jury is still out. Right now, he wants to save all of the people who can't afford his talent."

Chase shook his head, no longer fazed by his father's familiar refrain. It was one part annoyance, one part pride, and one part a reminder that the only reason Chase could represent poor clients was because his family had joined the ranks of the rich.

"Dad," was all he said, as he patted his father's back.

"Is your mother here?" David Laclede asked.

"No, when I left, she had a legal file spread out across the kitchen table. I'm here for work. I'm doing a story on Teen Alliance and the young man who is being honored."

"Ah, that would be Jarrett," Dee volunteered. "I sit on the board of Teen Alliance. They're an inspiring—and worthy—nonprofit. And I hope we can help Jarrett and other young people like him get the opportunities they deserve. We forget how much of getting into college isn't just about grades. You must know how to navigate the higher education system. There are applications, scholarships, and the dreaded FAFSA maze."

Dee stopped and smiled. "Sorry, when I care about something, I can go on and on."

"I don't mind at all," Debbie said, finding herself liking Dee despite her society status. "I've written quite a few stories about kids in similar situations. When I was young, I didn't realize how much I had leaned on my parents to guide me through the college process."

"You know I had the pleasure of knowing both your parents," David said. "Fine lawyers. Fierce opponents. Good people. I heard about your mother's cancer. How is she doing?"

"Nothing seems to rattle her." Debbie paused. "So far, she's been lucky enough to skip radiation before surgery. We won't know about chemotherapy until after her tumor has been tested. I'll let her know you asked about her. Now, I'm sure you all need to mingle. And I should really go meet up with Jarrett and his family. It was a real pleasure."

And she had meant it, much to her dismay. She wanted to dislike the society set. But the Lacledes seemed different. And David was nothing like she expected. He was much more charming than her mother had led her to believe.

"Miss Debbie!" Jarrett said as he saw the reporter approaching.

Hearing *Miss* in front of her first name was another reminder that St. Louis was situated at the intersection of the east, west, north, and south. The southern custom of children adding a *Miss* to the first name of an adult woman was one that still seemed to prevail in the African-American community.

"Hi, Jarrett!" Debbie couldn't hide her enthusiasm at seeing the happy young man. "Are you excited?"

"Aw, it is no big deal."

Jarrett's grandmother spoke up. "Hmm, no big deal. You sure fussed a lot getting dressed tonight, boy."

"This is my granny."

The elderly woman stretched out her hand formally. "I have a name. Ada Davis. I saw you at the funeral. Jarrett told me who you were," Ada said, shaking her head. "Too many babies dying. Too many babies locked up. This old woman's heart just can't keep taking the sorrow."

She stopped herself as she looked at her grandson. "Well, this is a night to celebrate. I am proud of my grandbabies. Jarrett was also such a bright child. And a handful. Seems like as soon as he could walk, he was getting his hands on everything in the house. It started with pots and pans. Then he moved to the television remote. Then it was lamps and cameras. He was always takin' things apart. I was always scolding him when I would look after him while his parents were at work. I asked him why he did it. You know what he said?"

Debbie shook her head. "What?"

"He said he liked puzzles. He had to take it apart to know how it worked. And he liked the challenge of putting things back together."

"Did everything still work once he was done?"

"Mostly," Ada said.

Jarrett laughed. "Yeah, I had some problems getting an old TV back together."

"My husband, Jarrett's granddad, he used to get ticked. But I told him hush. I figured that if taking things apart and putting them back together kept Jarrett at home and off the streets, it was a good thing. His mind was just craving something—and as long as he focused on old things, he wasn't doing too much harm."

"Yeah, after I took the TV apart, Granddad decided it was time for a computer. He brought home a used one, something they were getting rid of at work," Jarrett added. "Once I had the computer to play with, I stopped messing with his things."

Ada nodded her head. "My husband was a wise man. He figured out a way to channel Jarrett's curiosity. And he had a vested interest in keeping his good television in one piece."

"Is your husband here?" Debbie asked.

"Yes, he is. He's looking down from heaven right now," Ada said. "He's been up there nearly ten years now. Lungs finally gave out. He worked at the cement factory most of his life. They mixed asbestos with the cement to make it stronger. Black workers were given the dirtiest job—offloading bags of asbestos from trains that pulled right up to the factory. Dust everywhere. And when the bags broke, he used to say it was like Christmas, snowflakes of asbestos floating around them in the air. Took a long time, but we got a settlement, part of some class-action lawsuit. But the money didn't do nothing to make the suffocating pain he endured any more pleasant. And then God called my true love home. Sometimes it is hard to thank the Lord when someone so precious isn't with you in the physical sense any longer. But I try to tell myself that the good Lord also gave me my man. And I had beautiful children. And," she smiled as she looked at Jarrett, "a clever grandson."

Ada, avoiding the wine on the table, reached for her glass of water and took a sip. "My husband," she said with a faraway smile, "he was always thinking about me—and about his family. He worked hard to pay off our home. That way I'd always have somewhere to live. What he couldn't have known was that crack cocaine would sweep through our neighborhoods like wildfire, claiming a whole generation of young people—much like heroin is doing now to white folks in fancy neighborhoods. But that's another story," she said, shaking her head again.

Ada wiped the sweat off the bottom of her glass carefully with a napkin, then set it back down on the table. "Those who could flee, well they left. But now I had a house that, if I sold it, wouldn't buy me a new one in a safer place. So, I stayed. Besides, someone's got to keep an eye on the next crop of babies coming up in the neighborhood. And when my time comes, it comes. And then I'll be with my husband once again."

She patted her grandson on the knee. "I'm an old woman, I don't care so much anymore about myself. But I'm so happy for my grandson. And his grandfather would be—is—so proud. Proud that his grandson would get to use his brain, not his muscle, to make a living. He'd be so proud to see all these people here, in their fanciest of clothes, honoring Jarrett."

Debbie willed away tears. This was material that she could weave into a riveting lead paragraph.

"I'm really honored that I could be here," Debbie said. "Most of the stories I write don't have happy endings."

Debbie's heart felt lighter as she left the fundraiser. Spending time with Jarrett, his parents, and his grandmother, watching Darlinda cajole just a few more donations for a worthy cause, had softened her reporter's cynicism.

Journalists looked for dark clouds, not silver linings. It couldn't be helped. They were the ones who kept the public advised of floods and tornadoes. They were the ones right behind rescuers and first-responders in the aftermath of a school shooting. And every journalist on the beat long enough had, at least once, been told a blatant and outright lie by a powerful person whose only concern was protecting his or her position, not the public good.

But tonight, Debbie had witnessed generosity and optimism. It had been a while since she felt so positive.

"You seem to be in high spirits, Ms. Bradley." The speaker was concealed behind a pillar at the hotel's entrance, only the bright blue sleeve of a uniform clearly visible. But she knew who was attached to the voice.

"What brings you here, Detective?" Debbie asked as Flannery stepped out of the shadows. Instead of his usual khaki pants and white button-down shirt, he was in a crisp uniform of bright blue, navy tie, navy pants, navy cap with a gold crest on the front, polished dress shoes, and a clearly visible gun strapped to his waist. A 9-millimeter Beretta, Debbie guessed, based on the knowledge she'd gleaned from a story she'd done while working in Washington about the Virginia owner of a shooting range who was fighting with local neighbors in exurbs over the noise.

"Because the mayor and police chief attended the gala this evening, we have some extra police presence. I agreed to take the spot of one of the young officers who was supposed to work. His wife went into labor earlier today. Their first kid. I had nothin' better to do."

He paused. "So, I take it you were here for, er, pleasure?"

Debbie shook her head emphatically. "This was all about work. But there was no blood involved tonight. While I'm not one for fancy affairs, I do like to see someone deserving receive some recognition for a change."

Flannery nodded. "I see. My idea of fun is bocce ball and a beer."

"You play on The Hill?" Debbie asked, referring to the traditional Italian neighborhood in St. Louis.

"Where else?" Flannery answered. He looked at the keys already in Debbie's hand. "Where's your valet ticket?"

"Valet. Seriously? I'm still waiting on my first paycheck."

Flannery frowned. "The area is already clearing out so there isn't a lot of foot traffic on the street. Why don't you let me walk you to your car? I was actually getting ready to head home. The mayor and chief ducked out about an hour ago. Because I did a favor, I got to be the first to get off for the evening."

"Really, that isn't necessary. I can take care of myself."

"Humor me," Flannery said, gesturing with one hand to encourage Debbie to proceed in front of him down the steps. "While I'm not a fan of reporters, I also don't want to see anyone hurt."

She wasn't a damsel in distress. She'd been in rougher neighborhoods by herself in pursuit of a story. But perhaps this was a chance to get to know Flannery better. She hadn't given up on turning him into a source. In fact, after Sam suggested it would be impossible, it had become a personal challenge.

"Fine. But if you're going to walk with me, you have to tell me a little bit about yourself."

"Off the record?"

"You might be surprised. I am capable of carrying on a polite conversation. Besides, I've worked enough tonight."

"Again, off the record?" Flannery asked.

"Of course," Debbie answered as Flannery fell into step beside her, shortening his stride to accommodate Debbie's high heels.

"You don't wear heels often, do you?" he asked.

"Why?"

"You're limping."

"If I wasn't worried about broken glass, I'd take these damn things off and walk barefoot."

"My ex-wife loved high heels. The more expensive, the better. Though I'll admit that her legs were the first thing I noticed when we met."

"So you're divorced. Remarried? Kids?"

"Yes, I'm divorced. Nope on the rest."

"A dog?" Debbie asked.

"Not even a dog. Although I do like them. In fact, my ex-wife and I had a dog. But she got it in the divorce. No, I work a lot. It just wouldn't be fair to leave a dog alone so much."

"A special friend?" Debbie asked.

Flannery laughed. "You sound like a grandmother. No. No special friend. I don't have time for that either. "

"So, work is truly your life?"

"I suppose," Flannery admitted. "But here's a bit of irony for you. My ex said I wasn't ambitious enough. She left me for a man who she thought had more potential."

"Harsh," was the first word that escaped from Debbie's mouth.

"Fair is fair," Flannery said. "Let's see how the interviewer feels about being interviewed. Is there a Mr. Debbie?"

"Complicated. A month ago, I was engaged. Now I'm not even sure if we're speaking to each other. He wasn't happy that I took a job in St. Louis to help my mother out for a while."

"Ah, I heard about your mother. Cancer," Flannery said.

"How do you know that?"

"C'mon, big little town, right? I know a lot of lawyers. And judges. You hear things. Once I read you were assigned to cover the crime beat, I figured I better know a bit more about you. You're not the only one who researches."

Debbie stopped in the middle of the sidewalk and looked at the empty space next to the curb.

"What?" Flannery asked.

"I could have sworn I parked my car right here," Debbie explained.

"Are you sure?" Flannery asked. "There's no broken glass," he observed. "That means it probably wasn't stolen."

Debbie pressed the unlock button on her key fob, waiting to hear a beep from her car. Nothing came. She held the key up to her mouth, using a trick she'd read on some random blog, to amplify the range, and pressed again.

"Um, Debbie," Flannery said, "did you see this no parking sign?"

"Yes," she answered defensively. "And I didn't park there. Not really."

"What do you mean, 'Not really'?"

"Maybe an inch of my bumper was over the line. But ninety-five percent of my car was parked perfectly."

Flannery sighed and shook his head. "It's that five percent that will get you in trouble every time."

Flannery took out his cell phone and dialed. What followed was a brief conversation that ended with the revelation that Debbie's car had been towed.

"Aw, hell!" Debbie said. Her feet hurt. She was tired. And now her car was gone. "What am I going to do now?"

"Come with me," Flannery commanded. It took another ten minutes to reach a police squad car, a white Ford Taurus with St. Louis Metropolitan Police lettered in blue and an image of the arch emblazoned on the side.

"Get in," Flannery ordered. "We're going to Ace Towing. I'll help you get your car."

"Don't you have more important things to do?"

"Probably. But I don't think that either the police chief or the mayor would be happy to hear about a reporter covering this good news event had her car towed. Plus, this doesn't make sense. A ticket? Sure. But towing?"

They stopped at a light, and he turned to her. "Look, off the record, I think someone exercised poor judgment; was a little too by-the-book. I'm not sure why. But I will get to the bottom of this. In the meantime, let's get your car back."

Flannery headed east, the police car passing under streetlights as he guided them through the deserted streets of St. Louis, a city that really liked its sleep. A police radio dispatcher broke the silence of the car ride. "Suspicious person reported at the 1900 block of Rutger," the dispatcher announced. A police officer replied, stating he was in the area and would head over.

Debbie leaned against the headrest and shut her eyes. "That's near my mom's house."

"I wouldn't worry," Flannery said. "That's a good neighborhood. When someone is walking around late at night that the residents don't recognize, they call." He paused, then when she didn't respond, asked, "Tired?"

Unaccustomed to a soft tone from the gruff policeman, Debbie regained her focus. "Yes. I had been looking forward to going home, getting out of these shoes, and crawling into bed. It has been a very long week."

"Hopefully, this won't take too long," he replied before lapsing back into silence.

Flannery turned into the entrance of what appeared to be an abandoned industrial park. There were a few crumbling red brick buildings that had boards in the gaps where glass windows had once been. There were spray-painted messages scrawled on the crumbling walls: "Super," "LDS," and "RatFag."

As they drove on past the decay of a once-thriving cluster of manufacturing buildings and warehouses, there was a ten-foot chain-link fence topped with barbed wire. Inside the fence, Debbie could see cars lined up in rows. Some were battered, others had cracked windshields, and several had crunched front ends. But Debbie noticed that some of the vehicles were in perfect condition. Others were covered in a thin layer of grime, the dust of the gravel road that had been kicked up and blown over the vehicles. They were the ones that had probably been there awhile, the owners unable to gather the money to get their car out of hock, and with each passing day, further in debt.

The parking area allocated for visitors was small—more of a begrudging afterthought for those who, like Debbie, weren't happy about being there in the first place.

Flannery stopped the cruiser, and the pair got out. "I think it would be best if you let me do the talking," he advised.

A cheap bell clanked against the front door when it was opened. A man with thin, oily hair that had once been black, but was now a shade of dirty gray, sat behind the desk. The fluorescent lighting did little to flatter his waxy skin. He had a pencil in one hand and a find-a-word puzzle book in the other. An ashtray with a mound of yellow butts lay on the desk, near a Styrofoam cup with brown liquid. Cold coffee, Debbie guessed. A small fan on the desk hummed as it turned from side to side.

"Yep?" the man said without looking up from his puzzle book as Debbie and Flannery entered.

"You've got a car here—a Honda Civic—that should not have been towed," Flannery said gruffly.

"We got a lotta Civics," the man said, looking at the officer in front of him, unimpressed by the uniform.

"It came in this evening. Towed from the Central West End. Dark gray."

Flannery looked at Debbie. "Do you know the, license plate number?"

Debbie shook her head. "No, not off the top of my head, but I haven't had it titled yet in Missouri. It has Virginia plates."

The man scratched his head, the greasy strands of hair clumping together when they touched. "Not ringing a bell."

Flannery's jaw tightened. "What's your name?"

The man put down his puzzle book and stood up, his shirt stretched tight against a protruding belly, stained just below the neck with something that Debbie guessed was grease from a takeout hamburger. "What's it to you?"

Before the man could say another word, Flannery reached down to the desk and started shuffling through piles of paper before he seized a memo addressed to Quinn Hawkins.

"Ms. Bradley, would you like to get out your reporter's notebook and interview this man? Maybe you could find space for a piece in your magazine about your visit to a towing company that also serves as an impound lot for the city police?" Flannery asked. "I'm guessing his name is Quinn; Quinn Hawkins."

"I'm not talking to a reporter. And I'm not talking to you," he said defiantly.

"Are you saying you're refusing to answer my questions? How good would that look if the towing lot the city has a contract with is subject to bad press? What's the mayor going to say, Quinn?"

The man sat down behind the desk and shuffled the stack of papers that Flannery had just been rifling through. "I found it. A Honda Civic. Virginia license plates." Hawkins picked up the phone. "I want you to bring that Civic up front, the one that came in tonight." Hawkins paused. "Yeah, with Virginia plates." He paused again. "I don't care. I said now."

Debbie studied Flannery as she listened to Hawkins's one-sided phone conversation. He never raised his voice, he didn't draw his gun, he just sized up his opponent quickly, diagnosed the sensitive spots, and applied pressure in those areas to get the information he wanted.

Hawkins hung up the phone. "Wait outside. Someone will bring the car around in about fifteen minutes."

"Don't make us wait too long. Otherwise, we'll be tempted to stretch our legs and take a look around," Flannery said matter-of-factly.

She wasn't in trouble. But Debbie still couldn't shake that uneasy feeling that comes with seeing a police cruiser in the rearview mirror.

Flannery had insisted on following her home to ensure she made it safely, saying he wanted to make sure her car hadn't been damaged or tampered with by the tow lot. So now she was scrutinizing her speedometer and resisting the urge to roll through the four-way stops that dominated the city's side streets. Even though the streets were empty, Debbie came to a complete stop each and every time.

Finally, she pulled up to her parents' Painted Lady. There was a two-car detached garage in the alley, but her mom hadn't cleared her gardening paraphernalia from one of the spaces for Debbie. And since the other side was reserved for Beth's beloved Tesla, it was street parking for Debbie. Just like back in D.C.

Flannery lowered the driver's side window. "Nice house."

"Yeah, it is," Debbie agreed. "This is where I grew up. I'm back in my old room for now—until I have the time and energy to find my own place."

"If you need any safety information on the areas you're considering, let me know," Flannery said.

Debbie nodded, once again caught off guard by his offer. "Look, thank you for helping me. And you saved me a lot of money, money I don't have right now, to get my car out of a tow lot."

Unable to say *you're welcome* because he wasn't comfortable with gratitude, he merely nodded before muttering, "Well, good night."

Debbie walked the steep front steps up to the front exterior door. She unlocked it, stepped onto the marble floor of the tiny alcove, and then unlocked the interior set of doors—a common feature of the Victorian architecture in Lafayette Square. Debbie gave a small wave to Flannery to let him know she was inside, feeling like a schoolgirl who'd been dropped off at home by a friend's parent.

Once she was sealed safely inside, Debbie tossed her keys into a clay bowl that sat on top of a vintage walnut side table, hearing the oh-so-familiar clunking sound, one she'd known since she was a child. The bowl had been something her parents had picked up on a trip to Mexico many, many years ago, in the days before Debbie existed. They'd used it as a key bowl since before Debbie was born. Debbie used it once she started driving. And now she was back home, slipping back into familiar patterns.

She climbed the stairs to the second floor. At the top of the landing was a central room that served as a lounging area for the three bedrooms situated there. Debbie discovered her mother dozing on the couch, a laptop open on the coffee table. The screen had lapsed into sleep mode.

"Mom," Debbie said, nudging her mother's shoulder softly. "Mom."

Beth stirred and then stretched her arms. "What time is it?"

"Time for bed," Debbie answered as she picked up the notebook with her mother's scribbles and set it down on a nearby coffee table.

"How was the gala?" Beth asked.
"Eventful, very eventful."

7 DISTRACTIONS AND DESTINY

The morning after the fundraiser, Debbie felt as if her skull was being stretched outward. It didn't feel good, not one bit. It wasn't a hangover. She hadn't had a drop of alcohol the night before. In fact, it was one of her strict rules: Don't drink while working. She often picked up a wine glass and pretended to sip, just to blend in with the crowd. For some reason, a drink in her hand seemed to put the drinkers she was interviewing at ease. But she knew that halfway into a generous pour, she risked getting too chummy, too chatty. And that could be dangerous.

Coffee, Debbie thought as she rolled out of bed, grabbing her favorite gray sweater. It was more of a wrap than a sweater, light enough to wear in the summer, but providing enough coverage over her pajamas so that she wouldn't scandalize the neighbors if she ventured out onto the back porch. With houses so close you could see into the neighbors' windows without trying, it was safe to guess that folks looking down from their second floor would easily be able to see into her backyard.

The sweater hung on the back of her bedroom door. She could still recall the day her father had put that hook up on the door. She'd argued to her parents, some twenty years earlier, that a hook would help keep her room neat. Her messiness had been a source of friction with her parents when she was a teen.

Squeezing the sides of her temples with her hands to try to push her skull back into place, Debbie stepped over the black heels that she'd dropped in the middle of her bedroom floor after getting home. She searched for a pair of moccasin-style slippers that were half buried underneath a growing pile of dirty laundry. Her mother's black cocktail dress was draped over Debbie's favorite navy overstuffed chair, the one she often curled up into with a book when she was a girl. Even though the dress needed to be dry-cleaned, Beth would have had a fit if Debbie had tossed it on the floor.

Debbie opened her bedroom door and entered the sitting room. Her mother's laptop was still on the coffee table. Beth's bedroom door was closed. Debbie hoped she was sleeping. The mastectomy was only a day away. Her mom's body could use the rest.

Debbie headed for the first floor, but it was no use trying to creep quietly down the stairs. The treads on the steps of the 120-year-old house would still pop no matter how softly Debbie tried to descend.

Old houses, like old ladies, refused to remain silent.

Debbie entered the kitchen and poured her first cup of black coffee. Holding the warm mug in her hand, she stepped outside to the wooden deck located just off the kitchen. Like most of the homes in the Victorian neighborhood, the backyard space was small. The next-door neighbor, wearing a white robe with a luxury brand logo, was watering her plants on the back porch. She waved at Debbie when she heard the back door open.

Even though the space was tight, Debbie admired her mother's ingenuity. Three raised vegetable beds were squeezed in the space just beyond the raised deck and a few feet in front of the detached garage. Large planters on the deck served as vertical growing spaces for tomatoes and cucumbers. In the tight areas along the six-foot-tall fence that surrounded the yard, Beth had replaced ornamental trees and shrubs with Missouri native flowers like black-eyed Susans and purple coneflowers; treats for the birds and bees that helped pollinate her garden.

Debbie removed a cover from one of the Adirondack chairs, sat down, and let her thoughts drift. A bright red cardinal landed on the wire that connected the power lines in the alley to the house and began to call, "Purty, purty, purty." When she was a little girl, her father had taught her to recognize the song of the bird that was as cherished by St. Louisans as their beloved baseball team.

She thought of Jarrett. Her story about the Teen Alliance honoree would be as sweet as gooey butter cake, another St. Louis tradition Debbie hadn't thought much about since she'd been away. Sam would complain about the sugar overload in her story, but even he had to admit that the readers might enjoy a break from the unrelenting negative news at home, in the nation's capital, and abroad. And the magazine owner might even take a bigger hand in helping engineer Jarrett's fate.

A female cardinal, with its brown coloring and warm red crest, landed near the male. Cardinals mated for life. Perhaps they were a couple, Debbie guessed, before they took flight together. *Christian.* His name popped into her head. She pushed it away by replacing it with work.

Jarrett and Joshua. Two boys growing up in the same area, only a few years apart in age. One was being lauded, another lambasted.

They weren't the only contrasts she'd encountered since coming home.

If Teen Alliance was an organization that tried to lift people up, Ace Towing seemed to pounce on people when they were down. Dingy, dirty, and depressing. The clerk, Quinn Hawkins, would never win a customer service award.

Debbie went back inside to refill her coffee cup and grab her laptop. She set it down on the kitchen table. Casenet, the online service of the Missouri judiciary, might have some information on Flannery's divorce. Debbie typed Daniel Flannery into the search field. He lived in the city, so it had to be in the courthouse in that jurisdiction.

Having grown up in St. Louis as the daughter of two attorneys, Debbie was already familiar with one of the metro area's unique quirks. There was no county for St. Louis city. St. Louis County was a separate jurisdiction, the result of the so-called Great Divorce in the late 1800s after farmers and city dwellers fought over the direction of the region. It was a fight that led to fractured government and myriad competing municipalities. In addition to the city of St. Louis, St. Louis County was now dotted with its own little cities— indeed, there were over ninety municipalities inside the county's borders. The more the area fractured, the further it slipped from away from its onetime archrival, Chicago. Just about the only thing that St. Louis now lorded over the Windy City was, of course, baseball.

Flannery vs. Flannery appeared on Debbie's screen. Because it was a divorce, the publicly available information was limited. However, it appeared that a Denise Flannery had filed a dissolution proceeding against Daniel Flannery a decade earlier.

Debbie opened another tab on her internet browser and typed in the search terms "Denise Flannery St. Louis."

Search results popped up on the screen.

According to a newspaper wedding announcement, after her divorce, Denise Flannery had married Jim Robertson, a lawyer and former cop.

"It couldn't be the same Jim Robertson," Debbie mumbled to herself as she searched the mayor's name. Another news item with a photo of Jim Robertson being sworn in, his wife Denise at his side.

"Huh," Debbie said, continuing her one-way conversation.

"What?" Beth asked as she plodded into the kitchen, looking for her own cup of caffeine.

"You remember Detective Flannery?" Debbie asked.

"Mmmhmm," her mother answered as she added milk and sugar to her cup. Debbie had inherited her love of black coffee from her father, not her mother.

"Well, could it be that he was married to the woman who is now the mayor's wife?" Debbie asked.

"Denise Robertson? Yuck. She is just as phony and ambitious as her husband. From what I recall, the mayor was first a cop. Then he left the force for law school. He practiced for several years before running for mayor. No one thought he'd win. After all, he wasn't from St. Louis originally. California, I think."

"How'd he wind up here?" Debbie asked. St. Louis wasn't exactly known as a beacon for those who weren't from the area.

Beth shook her head. "I can't remember exactly. I think maybe he went to college here. Saint Louis University? As I think about it, I believe one of his parents was a university professor out west. Robertson was eligible for reduced tuition at several colleges. Saint Louis University was one. And he decided to get as far away from California as possible. Then he decided to stick around. Joined the St. Louis Metropolitan Police Department. Then after a few years, went to law school. Was a corporate lawyer—then won a long-shot race for mayor. I'm still not sure how he got the backing of the city's Democratic machine. Probably Denise. She's got that South City pedigree. Her family has connections to the unions and I think somebody, a great-uncle, was an alderman. Or maybe it was a second cousin? I can't keep track of all the incestuous machinations in city party politics."

"Interesting," Debbie said.

"Anyway," Beth continued, "I never met a couple who was more deserving of one another. How was last night?"

Debbie groaned and then related the story of the towed Civic.

"Ace Towing?" Beth asked. "I had a client who worked for them. He was entitled to file a work comp claim after he was hurt while trying to hook up a car to tow. He was hurt pretty bad. That can be some dangerous work. Anyway, he refused to pursue work comp, wanted to try to make a product liability claim against the maker of the tow truck's crane. I've never seen a man so reluctant to seek damages from his employer. He said his boss was good to him, he didn't want to mess it up. Even though I assured him that employers had insurance that covered these types of incidents, he insisted on leaving them out of the pursuit for compensation because they'd already been more than fair to him. But I never could find out if 'more than fair' converted into real dollars."

Debbie closed her laptop. Perhaps she was wrong about Ace Towing. Perhaps their shady exterior had her leaping to an undeserved conclusion.

"What are your plans for today?" Beth asked.

Debbie looked out the kitchen window, mulling over her options. She planned to take the day off for her mother's surgery, so it made sense to get a draft of the story on Jarrett knocked out. But she didn't want to be insensitive. Her mother might want a distraction.

"I'm not sure," Debbie answered. "And you?"

"Work," Beth said. "I'm going to be drugged up for the next couple of days. I better get ahead now."

"Mom, you should rest."

"C'mon. You were thinking of doing the exact same thing as me. Working."

"Well," Debbie started to say before deciding it was better not to lie. "Okay. You're right. I'll shower, send my editor an email updating him on the events of last night, write, and try to exercise."

"A productive Sunday," Beth said as she headed out to the porch to enjoy her cup of coffee.

After showering and dressing in an old pair of Levi's, a loose white T-shirt, and a pair of fluffy socks, Debbie was ready to get to work. Or so she thought.

Her headache was gone, replaced with a mild sense of dread that lurked just at the edge of her consciousness. It was always there when she needed to start a writing project. The story she had been drafting in her mind would never match up to the one that sputtered out in fits and starts onto her laptop screen.

She took a deep breath and opened a blank Word document, hoping to get down an outline that would effortlessly turn into scene snippets and rough paragraphs that could be massaged. But starting was always the hardest. She had to make readers care in the first couple of paragraphs. Otherwise, they'd lose interest and stop reading. The only ones who would slog through to the end were Jarrett, his family and friends, and Darlinda Owens. And Debbie's mother, of course.

There was some additional pressure that was making her freeze. She needed to prove herself to her peers. Christian might also be stalking her professionally, just as she was lurking around the edges of his online presence. Did he wonder how she was doing without him? A strong story would let him know that she was just fine.

As she stared at her screen, an email alert caught her attention.

"Shots Fired—58XX Pawnee Ave." Debbie opened the email. The report was fresh, just ten minutes old. Debbie clicked on the map to find the location, then used street view to take a look around the area.

It was a residential street with houses lining both sides. On one corner stood an abandoned apartment building. The red-brick structure looked to be from the 1920s or 1930s. A portion of the room visible on the front of the building had collapsed. The doors and windows on the first floor had been boarded up. A sign warning away trespassers had been posted. The upper windows were deep holes. The front yard was overgrown with weeds, and ivy had climbed from the ground to the roof in one portion of the facade.

And yet, the house next door was well kept and in good repair, at least when the street was photographed by Google. The neighboring lawn meticulously mowed. A hedge separated the two properties, and it appeared the homeowner was making every effort to keep the diseased property at bay.

Another email alert flashed on her screen. "Person down." Same general address. Debbie thumped her pen a few times on her reporter's notebook as the adrenaline rush began.

It was just too hard to stay away from the action.

It had become Debbie's new normal: flashing blue lights and a small crowd of people gathered behind yellow crime scene tape.

Debbie approached a young woman clad in tan shorts cut high, making the most of her shapely legs, and a red tank top revealing strong arms. She was standing on a patchy, yellowed lawn across the street from the abandoned apartment building that Debbie had glimpsed from her laptop. The woman, who couldn't have yet been thirty, was gripping the hand of a little girl with tiny braids sprinkled with white and red beads who looked to be about six.

"Hi," Debbie said in her least threatening voice. "I'm a reporter. I was wondering if you could tell me what happened?"

The woman looked down at the girl, whose wide dark eyes surrounded by long lashes never strayed from the crime scene unfolding in front of her.

"My daughter, she stayed with her auntie last night. I had to get her this morning. I stay just a few houses away from my sis. We was walking back home, me and my kid. That's when we heard shots. Bam, bam, bam. I just wrapped myself 'round her tight to protect her from slugs. Fool, can't he see there's children here before he decides to pop a cap?"

Debbie nodded. "Did you know the shooter?"

The woman eyed her warily. "Don't want my name in no paper. We mind our own business around here. I got a baby to take care of."

"I just want to hear what happened. I won't identify you."

The woman narrowed her eyes, looking Debbie up and down, and continued, "That broken-down place over there," she said, using her chin to gesture to the vacant apartment building, "it's no good. Neighbors have been hollerin' at the alderman and the mayor to tear it down or get the landlord to fix it up. But nobody listens. Landlord's prob'ly paying off the alderman. All I know is that bad people seem to hang around it."

The woman tugged the hand of the little girl. "C'mon, Destiny, time to get home," she said as she noticed Officer Parker heading for them.

Debbie surveyed the scene, taking notes of the action, as Parker made her way over. A cop wearing a green security vest leaned against a white squad car, puffing a cigarette. Several officers were gathered near the vacant building. Some were dressed in their uniform blues, others wore khakis and a black vest with white letters identifying them as St. Louis police. The female officers had their hair swept up. Many of the male officers had shaved heads or military-style crew cuts. Except for one. Flannery's thick, dark hair stood out, making it easy for her to pick him out of the sea of law enforcement officers who had surrounded the body draped in a white sheet next to the sidewalk. It appeared that the person down was next to a tree. Had the individual been standing there when shot, or was this where the victim dropped after running?

"I guess I'm not surprised to see you here," Parker said. "I was going to text you."

"What happened?"

"Ask anyone standing here, and they'll say they have no idea. But they know. They're just protecting the bad guys. As usual. My guess is that this was drug-related. The victim was standing next to that tree over there, near the apartment building. People on the street know it's a popular place to buy street drugs: heroin; K2, a synthetic cannabis with some very nasty side effects; hydrocodone; Oxycontin; cocaine; meth."

Parker continued, "A car sees someone standing next to the tree. The car stops. The person under the tree goes up to the car. Money, drugs exchange hands. The car drives away. We don't know yet if that's what happened here. Without any businesses around, we don't have any security cameras to check. There may be some neighbors with cameras or doorbells with eyes, but I doubt it. So we hope that the shell casings will tell us more. I think there were two guns involved. We found .45 caliber shell casings and .223 shell casings. Problem is that if the victim had a gun, it isn't anywhere to be found now."

Debbie crossed her arms. "But if this is an area where there's already a lot of criminal activity, couldn't it be that the shell casings are from earlier shootings?"

Parker shrugged. "Perhaps."

Flannery approached. "Officer Parker, I see you've found Ms. Bradley."

"Yes, sir. I knew you'd want me to keep an eye on her for you," Parker answered.

"You two seemed chatty," Flannery added.

"Yeah," Debbie answered, "if you call a bossy cop explaining to me yet again crime scene protocol and the press as chatty."

"Why don't you go over to that TV crew, make sure the cameras don't get too close. I'll deal with Ms. Bradley," Flannery said.

As Officer Parker headed over to a news van with a large antenna that was just setting up, Flannery remarked, "I thought you'd have the day off, after your late night."

"I could say the same to you," Debbie responded.

Taking in her T-shirt, jeans, and deck shoes, Flannery added, "Not quite so fancy today."

Debbie shrugged. "I had planned on staying home and writing. I'll be away from the office tomorrow, so I wanted to get a jump on my work."

"But you couldn't stay away from a crime scene, right?"

"What happened? Drug deal gone bad?"

"No comment, you know that. Talk to the PIO," Flannery said.

"How about letting me buy you coffee Tuesday? My mom's surgery is tomorrow, but I'd really like to thank you for helping me out last night."

"Look, I have nothing against you, except for the fact that you're a reporter. There's no way I would've left you standing out on the street last night. And your parents have a good reputation around town. My lawyer relatives speak highly of them. But I don't really want to socialize. Besides, I've got to be in juvenile court."

Debbie's eyebrows rose. "This wouldn't be about Joshua Lucas, would it?"

"You know I don't have any comment. Good day, Ms. Bradley," he said as he turned to head back to the crime scene.

8 LONGING AND LONELINESS

Debbie stirred from her restless slumber. The scent of Christian's skin, mixed with his cologne, hung in the air. *Where is he?* She looked at the pillow next to her head but all that was there was an empty space. Wrapped around her body was his old flannel shirt.

Before Debbie escaped D.C., she grabbed his shirt from their closet and stuffed it into one of her bags. He didn't notice because he'd stormed out of their apartment after yet another argument over her plans to return to St. Louis.

She remembered that shirt was still tucked in her luggage the night before Beth's surgery. After returning from the crime scene, Debbie cranked out her story. To celebrate the draft, she and her mom spent a quiet evening watching TV, a nature documentary because both women were too distracted to follow a real plot. Then they went to bed, though neither slept. Debbie heard Beth pace across the bedroom floor. Beth likely heard Debbie get up and then sit down in her favorite chair to try to read.

Sometime around midnight, Debbie remembered that Christian's shirt was in her luggage. Sure, she had the diamond ring he'd given her that day in early April when they were admiring the cherry blossoms in D.C.'s Tidal Basin. But it was a cold stone. It didn't compare to the warmth that caressed the very core of her heart when she put on the clothes that still smelled of him. He had indeed once loved her.

And so it was his presence that she instinctively felt when the alarm sounded before four a.m. From the hum of water running through the pipes in the old house, Debbie knew her mother was already awake. Debbie dressed quickly. They were going to a hospital, not a party. What Debbie looked like wasn't a concern. And it wasn't long before the two women made their way in the dark to the garage behind the house. Neither said much. Debbie began the day missing the jump start of coffee. But because Beth had been instructed not to eat or drink, Debbie figured she could do without her caffeine injection, at least until her mom went into surgery.

And when they arrived, the check-in was efficient. The operating room and medical personnel were ready and waiting. It was amazing how efficient the medical system could be when profit was at stake. An empty OR and waiting nurses and doctors were bad for the bottom line. And so it wasn't long before Beth was whisked away, with the nurse promising Debbie she'd grab her once her mother had changed into her gown and had been prepped for surgery.

Debbie had barely gotten settled into her waiting room chair and read some of the latest breaking news on her phone when the nurse fetched her and led her back to the prep area, where several patients had been ushered behind their own private curtains.

"Don't worry," Beth said. "Everything will be A-OK. I got this. And I'm super cozy in this contraption," Beth said, referring to space-age blanket that had been draped over her body to circulate warm air.

Debbie tried to smile but only managed a grimace.

"Oh, and I have a surprise for you," Beth said, as her words started to slur from the powerful sedative she'd just been given. "I talked to Maurice, I mean Judge Jamison. He's in juvie now. Juvenile. Not Joshua's judge, but good resource. Good man. Tomorrow. Afternoon. Tuesday. You'll talk to him. Old friend of mine. And your dad's. Law school. Julie knows," Beth said, referring to her sister and Debbie's aunt, Julie Birnbaum. It was then that the nurse signaled it was time for Debbie to leave.

As Debbie headed back to the waiting room, she had to give her mom props. Beth was a master schemer.

"You should go home," Julie Birnbaum said to Debbie when she walked into the hospital room.

"Hi, Aunt Julie," Debbie said, accepting a hug from the woman who resembled her mother.

Julie was Beth's older sister. Even though the two women had grown up in the same household, Debbie often wondered how they could be related. Her aunt lived a comfortable life in an outer St. Louis suburb. Julie had gone to college and gotten married shortly after graduating; she stayed home and raised the kids, headed up PTA, and was the go-to volunteer at her church. Julie was the type of mom who decorated the house for every holiday and never had to run to the Halloween costume store on October 30. Beth had been the reverse sort of mom.

The two sisters also sat on the opposite ends of the political spectrum. Julie was a conservative. Beth a social justice progressive. Julie attended Sunday mass. Beth preferred long walks in nature with her family on Sundays.

Even though Julie and Beth rarely agreed on anything, they managed to stay close. The biggest wedge had been the 2016 presidential election. As with so many families, it had been the most divisive event the two women had lived through. Eventually, they crafted a way through the minefield by building a path over their differences—which meant never ever discussing politics, world affairs, or climate change. Social media had proven more complicated. Debbie often heard her mother groan about her sister's latest post. And Debbie was sure her aunt wasn't happy about the news items her sister shared.

In short, Debbie had decided, Beth and Julie were like most Midwestern relatives, just trying to get along.

"Here," Julie said, pushing a brown paper sack into Debbie's hands, the type of gesture that didn't consider refusal a possible answer. "Bread Co."

Debbie smiled. Only in St. Louis was the fast casual restaurant known in the rest of country as Panera still referred to by its original name before a merger, St. Louis Bread Company, or the local shortened version, Bread Co.

"How's she doing?" Julie asked as she pushed a gray strand of hair behind her ears.

"Right now, she fades in and out," Debbie explained. "The morphine they've given her makes her loopy. But the doctors said the surgery was a success—whatever that means. It was a complete mastectomy, of course. And they removed the tumor and took a little extra bit of healthy tissue just to be safe. They took some lymph nodes for further testing."

Julie walked to her sister's bedside. "Poor thing."

Debbie smiled. "You better not let her hear you say that."

Beth started to rouse. She opened her eyes. "Water?"

Debbie grabbed a cup of ice and scooped out a few small chips. "Here, Mom."

Beth took the ice and then looked at her sister. "Make Debbie go home."

Julie smiled. "I'm working on it."

"Look, I'd really like to stay," Debbie argued.

"You're just going to annoy your mother if you stay. She wants you to go home and rest. The longer you remain, the crankier she'll get. I don't enjoy dealing with my sister when she's irritated. I'll stay. I've got a nice big book to read. You go."

Beth's eyes moved to her daughter. "Please?"

"All right," Debbie sighed as she picked up her laptop.

Julie reached into her purse. "I almost forgot. Here's your mom's instructions about the interview tomorrow with Judge Jamison."

Debbie reached for the paper and looked at her mother. Beth's eyes were closed but her lips couldn't help but form the shape of a satisfied grin.

9 TRIALS AND TRIBULATIONS

It was the dark circles around Maurice Jamison's eyes that Debbie first noticed as she was ushered into the judge's chambers by his assistant, a woman in her mid-forties with slightly sagging shoulders and lips that drooped at the corners.

"Come in, come in," the judge said, only briefly looking up from a legal file. Returning his concentration to the pieces of paper in front of him, Jamison gestured with his arm to a chair across from his desk. "Please, take a seat."

The assistant hustled out of the office.

Debbie remained still. When she was a kid, and there was a day off from school, her parents often took her to their law office. Sometimes that meant going with them to court while they filed documents or stopped in for a quick chat with a judge.

"Judges are busy. Their decisions have consequences," Cary explained to his daughter when Debbie complained about the rudeness of judges. "If they're in the middle of a thought or analyzing some problem, they need to finish it before turning their attention to a new issue. All day long, people are streaming in to interrupt them. Besides," he added, "I consider the silence an opportunity; a chance to recharge my brain for a few minutes by letting it rest."

Years later, Debbie realized her dad was using the time for micro-meditating, even if he never, ever, not in a million years, would have described it that way.

Those courthouse visits also taught Debbie to be comfortable with silence. As a reporter, she leveraged the unease her interview subjects experienced during lulls in the conversation. People felt compelled to fill in the spaces left by a long pause. That's when they'd start rambling—and sometimes revealing important details or uttering a sound bite that they'd later regret.

For Debbie, those verbal streams uttered by interviewees to fill the silence often created magical moments for her stories.

While Jamison reviewed the documents, Debbie studied the physical trappings of his office inside the building that was both a courthouse and a detention center for kids. There was a plaque from Legal Services of Eastern Missouri that recognized him as an equal access to justice champion, as well as a resolution passed by the St. Louis Board of Aldermen to honor him for his innovative work with juvenile offenders that had helped reduce repeat offenses and improved community relations. And there was a Legal Legends award from the Mound City Bar Association, one of the oldest black bar associations west of the Mississippi River. Before he was a judge, Jamison had served as its president.

"You're Cary and Beth's kid. I've heard a lot about you," the judge finally said, looking up from his file and taking off his glasses, smiling when he mentioned the names of Debbie's parents.

"Yep, that's me," Debbie said, still not knowing how to respond to links to her parents.

"I suppose your mom told you that your dad and I were close friends in law school. Sometimes I helped your dad get through a class. Sometimes he helped me. Your dad was one of my groomsmen. I was one of his. Your parents wrote letters on my behalf when I decided to put in an application for a judgeship. They also called some very important city politicians to help me out. I know you and your mom lost an amazing man when Cary died. But the St. Louis legal community also suffered a loss, we're poorer without his presence. And I'm sorry to hear about your mom's cancer. She's tough. She told me she's going to get through it."

"Thank you," Debbie said. She'd been away from St. Louis a long time. Away from people who had known her parents. In some ways, coming back brought Debbie closer not only to her mom but also her dad.

"Lord knows she's stubborn," Debbie added. "Cancer will have a tough time beating her."

The judge laughed. "And your mom has mellowed considerably. Man, was she argumentative and combative in law school. I think that is what attracted your dad to her in the first place."

It was funny, she never thought of her parents as young. Beth and Cary had always been Mom and Dad. But yes, they had once been struggling students trying to survive law school and then trying to carve a path into the courthouses of St. Louis. The fact that they did it together, and built a firm all on their own, was impressive. Even Debbie had to give them credit.

And, Debbie realized in a brief moment, she'd probably left St. Louis to get out of their shadow; to make it on her own. She became a reporter to be her own person. And somehow, she was finding herself being pulled back into her family's orbit.

The judge grasped the eyeglasses he'd laid on the desk and slid them back on his face. "I understand you're working on a story about a boy in juvenile detention facing some serious charges," Judge Jamison said.

"Yes, your honor."

"Let's talk off the record, okay?" Judge Jamison requested.

"Certainly," Debbie said, putting down her notebook.

"I never talk to reporters. But I respect your parents. They're honorable people. I'm going to assume, because they're your folks, that you got a double dose of integrity. Don't let me down, okay?"

Debbie nodded. She wasn't planning on breaching confidentiality. But now, she was even more invested in shielding the conversation because the judge had invoked her parents. She wasn't going to betray her mother or her father, or tarnish their reputations.

Jamison continued, "We're seeing an uptick in the number of young people here in juvenile court who've been out joyriding in stolen cars. It's dangerous. Dangerous for the public and dangerous for the kids. Someone was bound to get hurt. Unfortunately, we have an innocent dead teen. I can't tell you why we're seeing more of these cases," Jamison said, rubbing his forehead. "But I can tell you this: I want it to stop."

Debbie nodded. "Many people would agree with you. I went to the victim's funeral. The pastor called it babies killing babies. And I've heard the same thing from older people who live in the community. They're all fretting."

Judge Jamison said, "If you write a story, maybe it will help shine a light on this problem. Maybe the police will put more feet on the street. Of course, I'm in a sensitive role. Granted, I'm not handling the case of the juvenile you're investigating but I am a representative of the bench. I can't give you confidential information. However, I can point you in the right direction so that you can find public information."

Debbie took a deep breath. She parsed his words. He'd give her hints but she'd have to work hard to get the information. There was no way he was going to hand over juicy bits in a neat package wrapped with a tiny bow.

The judge continued, "The police department keeps stats on juvenile offenders. You could even manually add up the number of incidents on the daily crime reports published by the department. You've probably seen them. The SLMPD's crime and happenings report. If you could compare this summer's numbers to last year's, I think you'll see a big uptick."

"What about Joshua Lucas? How does he fit into all this?"

Jamison shrugged. "As I said, his case isn't on my docket. And you're a witness. So you're tap dancing on an ethical minefield. But, as you know, the boy is in some serious trouble."

Jamison sighed and rubbed the back of his neck. "His poor grandfather."

"Grandfather?"

Jamison continued. "At least his grandfather hired Chase Laclede."

"Well, what do you think of Chase?"

"He's smart. Like you, a product of a lawyer marriage. He's still needs a bit more breaking in. He needs to be knocked around a bit more in the courtroom so he can lose that tinge of smugness that gets coated on those private school boys in St. Louis. But he's idealistic. Thinks he can change the world. The injustice and unfairness in society hasn't battered him down yet. We need people like that. Although, if he stays in this line of work long enough, lawyers usually either become bitter because the rules don't get applied evenly to everyone, or he'll detach, adopt a gallows sense of humor, and erect a thick shell because it makes it easier to deal with human suffering, especially children. Not everyone falls into those two categories, but most do. And some end up bailing altogether, deciding that if they can't make a difference they may as well cash in and defend corporations."

"What about Detective Flannery?" Debbie asked. "What's he like?"

"Dan?" Jamison hesitated. "Straight shooter. Clean. By the book. Maybe that's because it is in his nature, or if he messes up, he's gone. His family's roots go way back in this town."

"What do you mean, if he messes up, he's gone?" Debbie asked.

"Sounds like you have more investigating to do, Debbie Bradley," Jamison answered before standing up and reaching for a black robe that was hanging on a coat rack. "Unfortunately, my next hearing starts in a few minutes. I need to get out on the bench."

Jamison looked at the clock on the wall. "You know, rich kids get in trouble, too. But their parents have money. Those parents ship their kids off to in-house treatment facilities, or a boarding school, or pay a lawyer to make the mess go away. Poor parents—and grandparents—are stuck inside the system. When they can't control their kids, they've got to call the police. And then they wind up here, and we try to get the kids back on track in a less-than-ideal environment."

He put on the robe and reached for a get-well card on his desk that he handed Debbie. "Will you give this to your mom?"

"Of course. I can't thank you enough."

"I've got one more favor to ask."

"Anything," Debbie answered.

"Take care of your mom for a bit. She's carrying a lot of weight on her shoulders. Not only her problems but those of her clients. If you help her, that's the best way to thank me."

Debbie had every intention of heading straight for the exit after leaving Judge Jamison's chambers. She would show him that she could be trusted.

But that was before she rounded a corner in the courthouse. An old man with snow white hair, clad in a white long-sleeved dress shirt and dark gray worker's pants, was talking to a boy dressed in a detention jump suit, red shirt, and red pants. A sheriff's deputy was standing next to the pair.

Debbie recognized the boy. She couldn't forget that face. It was the one she saw the day she flung open the car door of the Audi after it crashed: Joshua Lucas.

"You thought you was a big man," the old man said, his calloused hands trembling slightly. His voice sounding weary rather than outraged.

"Pop-Pop, I told you, just like I told the judge," the boy whined, trying to hold back tears. "I didn't steal the car. I found it. Near our house. The driver's window was broken. The keys were inside."

"Even if you're telling me the truth, that didn't mean you had to get in and drive. Last time I checked, you was too young to have a driver's license."

The boy looked down at his feet. "I know. I'm sorry. I know."

"I'm just glad your grandmother wasn't here to see this. When your momma got all hooked on crack, it hurt your ma-maw bad. When your momma died after your daddy shot her, I thought your grandmother was going to die, too. But you were her second chance. Thank the Lord in His infinite mercy and wisdom that she didn't live to see this day. She'd be so upset that the money she made me put aside for your college didn't go to school. She wanted so bad to see someone in her family go to college, just as she did. But instead, that money went to yet another lawyer."

Teardrops fell from the boy's face, leaving streaks on his cheeks.

"All right, time's up," said the guard who had been standing next to Joshua "Time to get you back. I'm not really supposed to let you stop here anyway. I only did it 'cuz your grandmother was the best teacher I ever had."

"Thank you, Elijah," Joshua's grandfather said to the sheriff's deputy.

"I want to go home," the boy pleaded.

"Hush now. You gotta be a man. You need to go with Mr. Elijah. I gotta talk to Mr. Chase. You be brave. Stay out of trouble. It'll only make things worse."

Debbie pretended to be looking at her phone as she eavesdropped on the conversation, trying to blend in with the caseworkers and lawyers who periodically passed in the hallway. Anything that would allow her to linger just a little bit longer.

"Sad, isn't it?" a voice said from behind Debbie. Her back stiffened.

"Detective Flannery, um."

"Don't bother explaining. I've been standing here a few minutes. You didn't even notice me."

"I," Debbie began, "it was an accident. I met with Judge Jamison. I was on my way out."

"But you just couldn't keep walking, could you?"

Debbie sighed.

"You know, if Joshua Lucas was half the man his grandfather is, he wouldn't be in this mess," Flannery said.

"He obviously cares about his grandson."

"Yes, he does. Did you know Ronald Lucas is a Vietnam vet? He was discharged with a Purple Heart. Went to work for the St. Louis School District as a janitor. That's where he met his wife, a kindergarten teacher in St. Louis public schools. She was one of those well-loved teachers who taught several generations of St. Louis kids. There's a school garden on the North Side named after her. She kept in touch with many of her students. She celebrated their successes. Unfortunately, her own daughter was a disaster. Crack. Joshua's dad shot Joshua's mom one night. He's still locked up. Joshua went to live with his grandparents. The grandmother died last year. The grandfather is all the kid has left."

"His grandfather sure didn't deserve this," Debbie said.

"Yep. And Rainaa didn't deserve to die either," Flannery answered.

Debbie nodded, as she recalled the image of the pink coffin and Rainaa's parents looking into it. *Who were the good guys and bad guys?* she wondered.

"What brings you here?" Debbie asked

"I told you on Sunday. I had court."

"Joshua?"

Flannery shrugged. "It seems like lately I can't seem to get away from you or the young Mr. Laclede."

"You're lucky, I guess," Debbie said. "Any news about that shooting on Sunday? The one on Pawnee?"

Flannery glanced behind him for a brief moment. "This is off the record, but the ballistics report indicates that the bullets from that shooting, the bullets that were pulled from the corpse, matched the gun that was used on Travis Hunt, that kid who was killed a few days earlier outside his mother's apartment."

"Really?" Debbie replied, too stunned by the revelation from the tight-lipped detective. "They were both drug dealers, right?"

Flannery shrugged. "So they say."

"Do you think this could be a gang war?" Debbie asked.

"Not enough info," Flannery said. "More evidence is needed. It is never wise to jump too hastily to conclusions."

Debbie decided to push her luck with Flannery. "What kind of gun?"

"The bullet casings that were found at the scene were a .40 Win S&W."

"Plain English?" Debbie asked.

"It is a bullet that was jointly developed by Winchester and Smith & Wesson. Popular with law enforcement and the personal defense fans," Flannery answered. "It would fit into a .40 caliber handgun, a gun that is easy to conceal and carry. As you know, each gun has a distinctive fingerprint."

"And you don't have the gun, right?" Debbie asked.

Flannery nodded. "No, it's missing."

Debbie knew she shouldn't question a gift. But she just couldn't help it. "Why are you telling me this?"

Flannery looked her in the eyes. "I'm not sure. You have a habit of showing up at every crime scene with your notebook, your phone camera, and a truckload of questions—I figure you might be one more set of eyes on the street that might help track down this gun. You're snoopy. A bit too snoopy. But people don't seem to have their guard up around you as much as they do a cop. Maybe you could be useful."

Debbie rubbed her forearm. "I see. You aren't trying to be nice. You just think I could be useful. And for now? Can I make it public that the same gun was used in both crimes?"

"Not so long as I'm your only source. If you find out in some way that is public, I can't stop you. But for now, no one should be hearing about this."

Debbie groaned. "The second most frustrating thing about being a reporter is having information you can't use."

"What's the most frustrating thing?"

"Having no information at all."

"It doesn't make any sense," Debbie said to her mother.

Beth, an impatient patient, had spent a little over twenty-four hours in the hospital. Sometime after the midnight following the surgery, she'd refused additional morphine.

"The last thing I need is to get hooked on drugs," Beth had declared to the night nurse and to her sister, Julie. The night nurse frowned. Patients who took their meds slept well. And sleeping patients were easy patients.

By the time the surgeon stopped by at about ten in the morning the day after surgery, Beth had shuffled past the nurses' station several times as part of her self-prescribed walking therapy. And when the surgeon arrived, Beth made the case that she should be released. She'd been mobile for hours, even with the pain. The surgery had gone well. She only needed one drain for her wound. She had no fever. And she'd rest better at home.

The surgeon relented, and Beth was home by early afternoon. Debbie found her mother asleep on the living room couch when she arrived.

"What doesn't make sense?" Beth asked, trying to focus on her daughter's words rather than the pain in her arm and chest.

"What Joshua was saying to his grandfather. The key was in the car and the window was broken. When I saw the car the day of the accident, the driver's window was shattered. I don't think it was shattered in the crash. The damage was mainly to the front of the car, not the side. So why would you break a window to steal a car if you had the key?" Debbie wondered.

"Interesting question," Beth replied. "What are some of the possible answers?"

"Maybe Joshua is lying about finding a key. Or maybe Joshua is telling the truth and he did find a key; perhaps he just likes breaking windows. Maybe the driver's window was broken in the crash and I'm wrong about that detail."

"There are some other possibilities," Beth said. "Perhaps the owner smashed the window to make it look like a stolen car, then left the key inside."

"That seems pretty farfetched," Debbie answered.

"Perhaps. But just spitballin' here. Did the car owner mention his key?"

"No. No he didn't," Debbie answered.

"Maybe he told the police, but he didn't tell you."

"I think I need to chat with him again," Debbie replied. "Try to get him to go over his story again."

10 BABY STEPS

If Sam Hitchens had a spirit animal, it would be a bear, one just emerging from hibernation. He always seemed cross and hungry, Debbie thought as she sat across from his desk, describing in one long monologue her interview with Judge Jamison, her eavesdropping on Joshua, and her conversation with Flannery.

"So, you got that tight-lipped detective to talk," Sam said while he doodled spirals on his reporter's notebook with a red pen. "He wants something."

"Maybe he likes me. Maybe he trusts me," Debbie suggested.

"Flannery doesn't like anyone. Especially reporters. And you haven't been around long enough to earn his trust. No. He's playing some sort of game. I just don't know what it is."

"You're paranoid. Although he did admit that I might be another pair of eyes that can help find the gun."

Sam put his pen down. "Just because I'm paranoid doesn't mean people aren't out to get me. Look, we're all using each other. He gave you that information because he wanted you to have it. Not because he wanted to make you an honorary deputy."

Debbie shrugged. "What do you want me to do, tell him to go away?"

"Hell no. Just be careful. He uses you. You use him. If it's a mutually beneficial relationship built on using one another, well, it is what it is. Just be sure you don't lose sight of the fact that the duty you owe is to the truth, not Detective Flannery," Sam said.

"I never forget where my duty lies," Debbie snapped. "So, what do you think of the story about Jarrett?"

"Puff piece. But I'll admit that I'm rooting for him even though we all know philanthropy is Febreze for rich people, they use it to get rid of the stench of corruption. Either that, or it's about status: See how rich I am because I can give so much away?"

"I don't think all good works are a sign of a guilty conscience or showing off," Debbie replied. "If you're successful, isn't it important to share the fruits with those less fortunate?"

Sam sniffed. "When good works come via a press release, it isn't about helping the less fortunate. You're probably just trying to rehabilitate a shitty image. Philanthropy is the modern version of sack cloth and ashes. Show the world just how pious you are. There's always an agenda."

"Geez. You're really negative today." Debbie frowned. "And you know, you are working for a magazine catering to the very people you're sitting here torching."

"It's like you and Flannery. They use me, I use them. So long as I don't lose sight of my duty, then that's the way it is," Sam said. "I'm a pragmatic cynic. And you know what? I just might be able to get some good journalism accomplished."

Sam picked his pen back up and resumed doodling. "Enough philosophizing for one day. Get in touch with the owner of the Audi."

Debbie nodded, knowing as she left Sam's office and headed back to her desk that getting in touch with Hank Frederich wouldn't be hard. She had a hunch she wasn't done with him so she'd already gathered quite a bit of background information.

Sifting through social media was a first stop for Debbie. Sure, some people found it an objectionable practice for a reporter to snoop a private citizen's online accounts. But social media didn't come with a reasonable expectation of privacy. Flannery must've known that because Debbie couldn't find a Facebook, Twitter, or Instagram for him. She doubted he'd be a Snapchat user.

But Hank wasn't Flannery. Hank's Facebook privacy settings allowed friends of friends to view his posts. Debbie discovered that they had a mutual connection; an acquaintance who'd been a high school classmate of Debbie's. They didn't hang out when they were teens, and judging by the woman's posts, they likely wouldn't be friends now. But Debbie tried to keep a wide swath of connections. You never knew when they would come in handy. Hank Frederich was a prime example.

Judging from his shares, he seemed to love his car, Cardinal baseball, grilling pork steaks on the weekend, memes about standing for the flag, locally brewed beer, and boating on Lake of the Ozarks. Divorced. No kids.

For more about his professional life, LinkedIn was her go-to tool. He was some sort of upper-level manager at a large reinsurance company. He began his career as an actuary and climbed the ranks. It was likely he pulled down a thick salary. He was probably someone who liked stats. He analyzed risk.

His Twitter profile was mostly abandoned. There were a few reshares of sports news. He probably didn't like the exposure on the platform. Debbie wondered if he had a profile on Reddit. There was nothing under his name, and it was too much effort, at least for now, to see if she could find him under a pseudonym.

Debbie dialed the phone number she'd found online for Hank's office. She knew that once he answered—if he answered—the clock started ticking. She'd have to intrigue him enough so that he wouldn't hang up before she got the answers she needed.

"Mr. Frederich, I have some information on your stolen Audi," Debbie began, without giving her name. She knew it was a bit of a cheap trick, but she didn't plan to quote him—yet. She needed information first.

"Yes?" he asked.

"Your car key: Was it missing when your car was stolen?"

"What? What sort of silly question is that? Who is this?" he demanded.

"This is Debbie Bradley, the reporter. We met the other day. I heard a rumor that the key was in your car when Joshua Lucas took it."

"I'm not missing my key. And I have the spare. And if the key had been left in the car, why was the steering column so badly damaged?"

"You're absolutely sure about the key?" she asked again.

"Of course. Who do you believe, a criminal or me?" Frederich said. "What else did the punk say?"

"Not much," Debbie answered. "He claimed he didn't steal the car. He said he found it, and the window was already busted out on the driver's side."

"Yes, another expensive repair. Obviously, if the burglar had the key, there would be no need to break the window."

"Do you have the car back yet?" Debbie asked.

"I talked to my repair shop yesterday. They're working as fast as they can, they claim, but it still isn't ready. And it took quite a while to get it from the tow lot."

"What was the delay?" Debbie asked.

"The usual. Evidence. The cops. Unhelpful clerks, not enough tow truck drivers to move it from the lot to the dealership," he said, sounding exasperated. "You name the excuse, and I'll have heard it."

"Thanks for your time, Mr. Frederich," Debbie said politely.

"Hey, how did you get my number?" he asked.

"I'll be sure to let you know if I learn anything else," Debbie said as she hung up the phone.

After jotting down her notes from the conversation, Debbie checked her email and found a surprise message from the prosecutor's public information officer, Michelle Lee, with a heading that read: "Probable Cause Statement."

The body of the email was professional, short, and cordial. The PIO was contacting her about the homicide of Travis Hunt. An arrest had been made, and charges were issued. The defendant, Roberto Simmons, would appear in court the next day.

The probable cause statement, a public document attached to the official charges, revealed that the defendant was twenty-two. The police claimed that the defendant acted with three other as yet unknown individuals in Hunt's murder. The statement claimed that the murder involved a dispute over drug territory. It also noted that the forensic analysis indicated that the murder weapon was a 40-caliber handgun. It didn't reveal that the handgun was used in another crime.

And there was a lead. The last known address for the defendant. It was incomplete—just a street name with the first two numbers of the four-numbered address of the house—but it was a start.

Debbie gave the probable cause statement a second read. Even though prosecutors file charges, police officers are the ones who are responsible for the probable cause statement and put a signature on the document. This one was signed by Detective Daniel Flannery.

Debbie picked up the phone and dialed the prosecutor's office.

"Michelle, this is Debbie Bradley," Debbie began. "I just wanted to thank you for the probable cause statement."

"You're welcome," Michelle said, full of professionalism and lacking warmth.

There was a pause as Michelle waited for Debbie to continue. *She's a pro,* Debbie thought.

"I was wondering if you could provide any additional details about the charges," Debbie said finally.

"I'm sorry, but we can't go outside of the probable cause statement," Michelle said firmly. "The prosecutors have to comply with the ethical rules. To protect a defendant's constitutional right to a fair trial, I can only provide as much information as what is in the public record."

"I understand completely," Debbie answered in her most professional voice. After all, Michelle was correct. And Debbie hadn't yet established the sort of relationship that would encourage off-the-record discussions. It was something Debbie knew she needed to do—quickly. Not only with the prosecutor's PR person, but also the public information officer who represented the police.

"Can you help me obtain a mugshot?" Debbie asked.

"Yes," Michelle answered. "Is it okay to send via email?"

"Perfect," Debbie replied.

"I should have it over in about ten minutes," Michelle answered. "Anything else?"

"That's it. I really appreciate your help," Debbie added before hanging up the phone.

Debbie pulled up the blog post she'd written right after the murder. It was more a blurb than a story. She'd simply update the first few paragraphs of the piece by noting that a man had been charged in the murder. And she'd note his age, his general address, and the fact that the remaining individuals were still unknown. The rest would stay the same. It was a piece that took fifteen minutes to update, plus the time spent attaching the mugshot and verifying the spelling of the names.

It was 4 p.m. when the piece was approved and uploaded to the website. Debbie sat back in her chair, tapping her fingers on the armrest. Flannery had known the information when she ran into him in the courthouse.

Perhaps Officer Parker could help her out.

Before Debbie climbed the cracked concrete steps with crumbled edges, she heard the wails of an angry child. The sound slipped through the iron bars covering the open front window that faced out onto the porch where a jumble of plastic toys were piled to one side. A pink Barbie convertible missing one back tire had been parked in the sink of a lemon-colored play kitchen that was streaked with dirt left after a summer storm.

Officer Parker had given Debbie the full address of Roberto Simmons, but she hadn't been happy about it. Debbie persuaded the officer to help her cause by conjuring up the image of a female reporter, armed only with a pen and notepad, knocking on the door of every single home on the block to find the friends and relatives of Roberto Simmons.

Debbie got her address. But now she knew that she owed Parker a favor.

There was no doorbell next to the front door, so Debbie rapped her knuckles as loudly as possible against the metal screen door, hoping that between her banging and the banging of the loose door against the metal frame, she'd be heard above the crying.

A young woman's voice shouted something that Debbie couldn't quite make out. A latch clicked and then the wooden door, dented in the places either feet or fists reached, opened slightly. Debbie looked down to see the wide eyes of a girl who couldn't have been more than five studying her.

"Momma!" the little girl shouted. "Some lady."

Debbie could hear cursing from inside the house and stomping across a wooden floor. The mother, who didn't look more than twenty-five, appeared with a crying baby clad only in a diaper on her hip.

"I'm sorry to interrupt you," Debbie began, trying to soothe the frazzled mother. "I'm a reporter with *River City* magazine. I'm trying to find out some information about Roberto Simmons."

"That deadbeat ass don't live here no more," the woman said defiantly.

"So you know him?" Debbie asked.

The woman shifted the baby from one hip to another. "The man who always leaves messes behind?" She placed a hand on top of her daughter's head and looked at the baby in her arms. "These girls don't need a daddy like that."

The child who'd opened the door wrapped her arms around her mother's leg.

"Do you know if he had any guns?" Debbie asked.

"I don't know nuthin' 'bout no guns. And even if I did know, why would I tell you?"

The woman took two big steps back into her home, pulling her children with her. The door slammed shut. The lock clacked.

Debbie sighed loudly. As she turned back toward her car, she caught sight of a curtain moving in the house next door. Someone had been watching.

Debbie mulled her options. She could retreat to her car, or she could approach the person who'd been spying. Retreat was a word she just didn't like.

The next-door neighbor's porch was tidy. A broom was tucked into a corner, and an outdoor mat had been placed by the front door. Pink geraniums in pots placed on the windowsills softened the look of the bars. A dark curtain betrayed the faintest tremble.

Debbie lifted the old knocker on the door and dropped it down three times.

"Go away!" a shaky woman's voice said from an open window that was covered by bars and draped with a curtain that hid her face.

"I'm sorry to bother you," Debbie said as she introduced herself as a journalist.

"I already heard your speech. I got nothing to say," the strained voice of an older woman said. "Do you know what happens to snitches? I don't want no trouble. And you should leave that girl alone. She's got enough problems taking care of those babies. If you knew what was good for you, you'd be gettin' on back to your car. Ain't safe for you to be wanderin' 'round asking questions that are none of your business."

"I'm just trying to find out about the man who lived next door," Debbie said.

"I don't know nothin' 'bout it."

"He may have been involved in a shooting. I imagine you were watching when the police arrived to arrest him. Do you know if they took any guns out of the home?"

The woman laughed. "Silly girl. No one owns a gun."

"But," Debbie stammered, "there's been gun violence in this neighborhood. People are getting shot. Someone has to own a gun."

"You don't know much, do ya?"

The window slammed shut. The conversation was over.

"You just missed my secretary," Beth said as Debbie entered the front door.

Beth was sitting on the couch, a stack of papers with yellow, blue, and pink Post-it Notes piled on the coffee table in front of her.

"Mom, seriously? You just had surgery. Don't you think you should rest a bit more?" Debbie remarked as she dropped her purse and keys at the front door.

"I'm fine," Beth said, even as she winced slightly while changing her position to face her daughter.

"Right," Debbie replied.

"I took a long nap and went on several short walks between the living room and the kitchen," Beth announced. "And then I went outside on the back porch. Got a little fresh air and walked to the garage and back."

"You should be resting, Mom," Debbie said.

"For me, this is resting," Beth answered. "If I were forced to Netflix all day, I'd go mad. Anyway, how was your day?"

"Unproductive and confusing," Debbie said as she summarized her day. "I can't seem to get anyone to talk to me."

"You have to earn people's trust, Debbie. Look at this from their perspective. They don't know you. You come into their neighborhood, ask a bunch of snoopy questions, demand answers, and then you get in your car and leave. Clearly, some fear retribution. They're the ones who must live with the consequences—not you. You get a story. They get harassed. Their loved ones may suffer. The limelight makes them a target. For some, they figure it is better to keep their heads down and fade into the shadows."

"I know. But I'm trying to help. And then I get lied to. People claim that no one owns guns in the area. Really? I'm not an idiot. Do you know how many 'shots fired' alerts I get daily from that area?"

"What if you weren't being lied to?" Beth asked.

"What do you mean? Guns are being fired all the time. I even heard a shot when I was walking back to the car. It was far off, but it was no firecracker."

Beth nodded. After all, she lived in the city and raised her child there. She also knew the distinctive pop, pop, pop of a firearm.

"Hear me out," Beth said. "The claim was that no one owned a gun. That isn't the same as saying no one used a gun or had access to a gun. The question you're asking is about ownership, not use."

11 THIN LINE

The young mom preferred grocery shopping early. The woman, her strawberry blond hair pulled back in a beige scrunchie, was dressed in snug yoga pants and a billowing T-shirt that fell below her behind. She hadn't imagined that it would be so hard to get rid of the last few pounds of baby weight, even after nearly two years of trying.

She parked her cart, stuffed with bags, next to the Ford Taurus that had been only a few years old when she got it before going off to college. Now, after marriage and a baby, the car was battered and worn, but it refused to stop running. The mom wiped cookie crumbs from her toddler's face, then fished her keys out of her purse, rummaging past tissues and boxes of raisins. After unlocking her car, she lifted her son out of the cart and buckled him into the car seat in the back.

"Okay. Now, just let me finish loading up the groceries," she said to her toddler before giving him the last bit of cookie she'd saved. Sure, it was only 8:30 in the morning, but sometimes a sweet bribe made her life a bit easier. Besides, a donut would be just as bad, maybe even worse.

When the mom turned back to her cart, two skinny white men in their twenties, wearing baseball caps pulled low on their heads, confronted her.

"Your keys," one demanded, holding a gun discreetly next to his body, aimed straight at her belly.

The woman backed up to shield her toddler.

"Your keys!" the man shouted.

The man's partner, looking around the lot, added, "Hurry up! Or we'll shoot you."

"Let me get my baby, and you can have my keys. They're on the front seat," the woman begged, as she turned to unbuckle her toddler from his seat.

"Security!" one of the men said as he reached for the woman's shoulder and yanked her back away from the car. "Get in!" he shouted to his partner while slamming the back door—with the baby still inside.

The mother screamed and clawed at the door handle that separated her from her child. The man with the gun aimed at the woman and fired.

"My baby! My baby!" the mother wailed as she bled onto the parking lot.

A single-file line of people wearing orange jumpsuits was ushered into the courtroom by sheriff's deputies. They entered through a door near the jury box and witness stand, one that was not open to the public. A deputy stood at the front of the line, gesturing the inmates toward the jury box seats. Another filed in at the end of the line, while a few more deputies were dispersed throughout the courtroom, positioned to keep an eye on the prisoners and to prevent family members, or victims who were sitting in the gallery, from getting too close.

It was an arraignment docket and Roberto Simmons, the man charged with killing Travis Hunt, was scheduled to appear.

Even though court proceedings rarely began on time, Debbie still arrived twenty minutes before the docket was set to start. She wanted to stake out the perfect vantage point—close enough to the front of the courtroom to maybe have a chance to listen to the sidebar discussions between the judge and the lawyers, as well as far enough in the back to eavesdrop on the muffled exchanges of the public in the gallery.

For that prime seat, Debbie chose the second row of benches behind the swinging doors that separated lawyers from the public.

A woman in her late twenties wearing a business suit, with long dark hair cascading smoothly down her back, entered the courtroom through the judge's door. Accompanying her was a fifty-something woman with faded blond hair and dark roots who wore dark blue slacks and a rumpled black sweater. She pushed a gray metal cart stacked high with greenish-blue files.

A young prosecutor and an experienced clerk with the prosecutor's office, Debbie guessed as she watched the two women and made a few notes in her reporter's notebook as she told herself, *I really need to cultivate more lawyer sources.*

The judge's clerk leaned toward the prosecutor and spoke in a tone too low for Debbie to make out. The lawyer glanced back at Debbie, exchanged a few more words with the clerk, and then the lawyer disappeared through the private judge's entrance.

Two more lawyers entered the courtroom from the public entrance. One of them was Chase Laclede, his right hand clutching a black leather briefcase. It looked nothing like the case her father had carried. The leather on the handle on her father's briefcase had worn away from years of use. The main section of the case was no longer a firm rectangle. Over the years, it had been stretched to the limit with files so that eventually, it was lumpy and misshapen. That briefcase still sat in the corner of her mom's office. The spot where she'd left it after cleaning out her husband's files following his death.

Chase smiled and nodded at the lawyers and legal staff on the exclusive side of the swinging door—the thin line that separated the audience from the actors. Debbie overheard the word *reporter*.

He hadn't noticed Debbie when he arrived. But now Chase turned and settled his gaze on Debbie. He set his briefcase down on the counsel table and made his way over.

"If I didn't think I was flattering myself, I'd say you were following me," Chase said as he extended his hand to hers.

Debbie grasped his hand firmly. "Maybe I could say the same thing."

"So what brings you here?" Chase asked.

"I've come for the arraignment of the defendant charged with murdering Travis Hunt, um, Roberto Simmons, I believe is his name."

"Simmons is my client."

"Really?" Debbie said. This was a piece of information she hadn't yet uncovered.

"I just entered my appearance in the matter a few moments ago. His family hired me yesterday."

"I don't suppose you want to talk about his case?"

"I do give you an A for effort, Ms. Bradley, but no."

"Well, what are you doing after the arraignment? How about grabbing lunch? Totally off the record."

"Can't. I'm booked solid. But my parents enjoyed meeting you. How's your mom?"

"She's at home. She's supposed to be recovering,"

Chase nodded. "I should get back to my work."

"Please consider lunch," Debbie said. "I'm not the enemy."

Just as Chase left, a woman in her late thirties wearing a navy pantsuit with a crisp white shirt, perfectly painted lips that were neither too bright red nor too soft pink, and a chestnut-colored bob made her way to Debbie.

"Excuse me," she said to Debbie, "I don't believe we've met."

"Debbie Bradley."

"Ah, *River City*. We've emailed each other; talked on the phone. I'm Michelle Lee, the public information officer for the circuit attorney's office."

"Oh, so pleased to finally meet you," Debbie answered, knowing full well that Lee was an important gatekeeper who could provide news tips, respond to sunshine law requests, clarify information, arrange interviews, and maybe slip her some tidbits on deep background. "Thanks again for sending over the probable cause statement in the Travis Hunt killing; the one that charged Roberto Simmons."

"Yes, that's right. That is today?"

"Yes," Debbie answered. "Say, you don't happen to know if they've found the other three yet, do you?"

The PR rep shook her head. "I would have to check."

"If you could do that, I would really appreciate it," Debbie answered.

"Sure, I'll take a look. In the meantime, if you have any other questions, please don't hesitate to let me know. Here's my card," she said. "Oh, and by the way, our office policy is that we don't allow prosecutors to talk to the press without my presence. So, just so you know, because if you do try to talk to one of them, they'll send you to me."

"I see," Debbie answered—while refusing to promise that she wouldn't still try to talk to the lawyers without the minder present.

"It isn't that we're hostile to the press. It is just that the ethical rules are tricky when it comes to public statements that may impede a defendant's Sixth Amendment right to a fair trial."

"But there's also a First Amendment right to free press," Debbie blurted out.

"Absolutely," the smooth-talking rep responded. "My job is to try to balance the First Amendment, the public's right to know, the defendant's Sixth Amendment right to a fair trial, and ensure the attorneys aren't disciplined or disbarred for running afoul of the ethical rules. I'm sure you understand."

"Completely," Debbie replied, trying her best not to betray her irritation with the rules of engagement that Lee had outlined.

As Debbie watched Lee leave, she noticed a familiar-looking face. It was the young woman with the two children whose door she had knocked on the day before.

The woman mouthed silent words to Simmons in the jury box. It took a few minutes before Debbie pinpointed the defendant—a stocky man with broad shoulders and a shaved head. The woman was pointing to her purse. A little girl sat on her lap. The young mother hadn't brought the baby. Perhaps she was asking for money, Debbie thought. The man shrugged and used his head to gesture toward Chase Laclede. Perhaps the money went to his lawyer.

"All rise," a bailiff commanded. "Court is now in session."

The judge, a woman with closely cropped silver hair and blue-rimmed glasses who appeared to be in her early sixties, entered the courtroom. Once she took her seat from the highest perch, the rest of the courtroom followed suit.

After a brief recitation of the courtroom rules, the judge nodded to the bailiff, who then read the first name on a printout. A man in the jury box stood up. His lawyer came forward, and the prosecutor quickly read off the charges. When asked by the judge how he would plead, "Not guilty," was the prompt answer.

Assembly line justice, Debbie thought to herself. Each person quickly going through the motions to get to the next stage in the criminal justice proceedings.

When Roberto Simmons's name was called, Chase Laclede maneuvered to the front, his smooth athletic movements a contrast to the lumbering, heavier attorneys. Debbie's mother had often talked about the toll the legal profession took on people. The stress and high stakes left some seeking solace in food, others found it in the bottom of bottle, some searched for it in a pill, and finally there were those who found escape in a series of extramarital affairs. The ones with less-than-healthy coping mechanisms were often easy to spot. It clung to their bodies; big bellies, yellowed skin, maybe a gaze that leered a bit too much at young women. Chase seemed fresh and wholesome in comparison.

The little girl, the daughter of Simmons, Debbie guessed, fidgeted on her mother's lap and waved when Simmons stood up. The mother quickly grabbed the girl's hand and pushed it down. Chase presented a memo that indicated his client was waiving the right to a reading of the charges and that his client was entering a plea of not guilty.

The judge looked at Simmons. "Is that correct? Do you wish me to enter a plea of not guilty?"

"Yes, your honor," Simmons responded.

The judge nodded. The arraignment was over in a matter of moments. Chase packed up his briefcase and headed toward the exit. He motioned to the mother and child, who got up and left the courtroom. Roberto, who had been escorted back to the jury box with the other prisoners, watched as his lawyer and his family left the courtroom.

Debbie felt her phone vibrate with a text message. It was from Officer Parker. An incident at a grocery store in South City. "Urgent," she had typed.

Debbie gathered her bag, shoved her notebook inside, and walked briskly out of the courtroom, darting past Chase's impromptu hallway conference.

In the corridor, she also spotted the back of a familiar figure leaving the prosecutor's warrant office. He was in a hurry.

Flannery.

The grocery store lot was crowded with police cruisers and television news vans, which forced Debbie to park her car on the residential street nearby. Usually, she was the only reporter at a crime scene.

Something big went down, she thought.

Debbie pushed through the crowd of people that had gathered and made her way to a TV camera operator who was waiting on a reporter to gather his notes.

"Hi. Debbie Bradley. I work for *River City* magazine. I'm new to town. Well, I grew up here. Just came back."

The camera operator nodded. "Yep. Crime Beat Girl. From D.C."

"News travels fast, doesn't it?" she said.

The cameraman shrugged. "You know what they say about St. Louis. Besides, our evening reporters are looking at your blog to get story ideas to pitch."

"Interesting. But you beat me to this one. What happened?"

"Carjacking," he responded. "Young mother with a baby."

"Geez!" Debbie said.

"Yep," he said. "The carjackers took the car—with the baby inside. And they shot the mother."

"Oh my God," Debbie said. "Is she...?"

"She's alive," the camera operator explained. "Fortunately, the carjackers were in a hurry or had bad aim—or both. They grazed her arm. She's gonna need stitches. The cops are searching for the bullet."

"What hospital?"

"She's still here. She says she's not leaving without her baby."

"What do we know about the guys who did it?" Debbie asked as the TV reporter who worked with the camera operator walked up.

The TV reporter, his notebook open, explained, "I was just asking about it. There were two men. White. Baseball caps. Right now, there's not much of a physical description. Medium height, thin build. That's about it.

122

The grocery store security folks and the police investigators are going to review surveillance tapes to see if they can learn more."

The camera operator chimed in. "Okay, we're about to go live."

"Thanks for your help," Debbie said as the TV reporter grabbed the mic.

If the mother was hurt, then the paramedics would probably be near her, Debbie reasoned. And the parking lot was so big, the scene so chaotic, Debbie was able to find a path to get near the ambulance.

The mother's eyes were red, her face puffy. Her hands trembled as she shooed away the emergency technicians who were trying to get her onto a bed. "No! I'm not going anywhere," she screamed. "What if they bring my baby back?"

Detective Flannery stood next to her. He grabbed a blanket from a paramedic and gently draped it over her shoulders, one firm hand lingering for a moment, as if he was trying to transfer some of his calm reassurance to the distraught woman. He sat down next to her.

"My baby," the woman cried as she rocked back and forth. Flannery sat still, his voice low. Debbie inched closer, trying to pick up what he was saying. With all the commotion of the TV cameras, as well as the growing crowd of shoppers-turned-spectators, no one had seemed to notice the print reporter.

"We're scouring the area," he said softly. "I have my officers searching Fillmore Park, just across the street. Carjackers want your car, not your son. They probably just panicked when they saw security. And we sent a police car to your husband's office. They're bringing him over right now to be with you."

The woman looked at the detective through tear-filled eyes. "I'm a horrible, horrible mother. I should never have put my baby in the car first. I should have paid attention to what was going on around me. That's what they always say. Pay attention."

Flannery placed his hand gently on top of hers. "No one expects this sort of thing. And besides, you may have saved your child. By strapping him into his seat, he's got some added protection. The fact you are here, instead of in that car, means we know what happened and we can flood the area with patrols. If you were in the car, there's no way you would be able to help him right now." He paused. "You're a good mother," he said emphatically.

The crowd parted as a man pushed through.

"Kevin!" the woman cried to the person who Debbie guessed was her husband. "Oh, Kevin!"

Officer Parker appeared. Debbie wondered if she'd escorted the husband. The scene was unfolding so rapidly that she couldn't be sure. "Detective, we may have found the baby."

The parents froze. Flannery, the mother, the father, and even Debbie stopped breathing for a moment.

"There's a car seat in the park with a baby strapped inside. The child seems okay," Parker said. "The patrol car that found him is on its way here."

At that moment, a patrol car with lights flashing and siren blaring pulled into the lot. The crowd fell back to let it pass. It stopped near the parents as the cameras converged on the scene. An officer opened the door to the vehicle.

The baby, spotting his mother, began to cry. The parents rushed forward. Ignoring the pain of the bullet, the mother wrapped her arms around the child. The father wrapped his arms around them both.

Flannery nodded to the emergency medical technicians. "Get all three to the hospital."
And with his back still to Debbie, he said, "Were you able to get all of that, Ms. Bradley?"

12 REVELATIONS

A medical exam is no day at the spa, no matter how many posters of beaches and mountains are plastered on the walls, Debbie thought as she sat with her mother, waiting for the surgeon to enter. Tranquil pictures sandwiched between biohazard waste containers, blood pressure bands, and medical glove dispensers weren't enough to make the space safe.

As they waited, the women knew there was a lot at stake. It was Beth's first appointment after her surgery. If everything went as planned, Beth would be getting the test results back on her tumor and lymph nodes. The insights from those tests would help decide whether chemotherapy was in Beth's immediate future.

To break the tense silence, Debbie turned to work. "You know, I still find it annoying that the mayor arrived at the grocery store parking lot just as the officers were bringing the toddler back to be reunited with his parents."

It was the day after the carjacking. And while the baby had been found, and the mother had already been released from the hospital, the two criminals were still at large.

"Mayor Robertson," Beth said, shaking her head as she sat on the exam table, a gown wrapped tightly around her. "If there's good news, and the cameras are rolling, he'll shove everyone out of the way to bask in the limelight. Now, I guarantee you that if things had taken a turn for the worst, Detective Flannery would have been pushed in front of the microphones and forced to explain the situation to the public."

"You're probably right. Although I suppose I shouldn't be too quick to criticize," Debbie admitted. "My story about the carjacking and kidnapping got a lot of hits on *River City*'s website. It's pinging around Facebook like a pinball. And Flannery should be sending me a big thank-you for that moving photo I got of him comforting the mother."

"Did you have to lead with *every mother's nightmare*? Kinda sensational, don't you think?" Beth asked.

Debbie shrugged. "Hey, isn't it every mother's nightmare? Moms lug their kids to the grocery store all the time. My readers can easily imagine themselves in the same situation."

Beth sighed. "I suppose. I have to say that Detective Flannery is rather striking. The photo was a good choice. I thought he'd look much grumpier, based on your description of him."

A light knock on the door ended their discussion.

The surgeon, a tall brunette with shoulder-length hair, strode into the room. She carried a file in her left hand and used her right to shake Beth's hand first, then Debbie's. She sat down on a roller stool, pulled up a screen on the computer, and opened the chart she'd carried into the meeting. The movements were quick. She was used to the ritual. She also skipped the small talk. There was a time for chitchat, but now was not one of them.

Beth's face didn't betray any hint of anxiety. Debbie wondered how her mom stayed so calm when her own stomach dropped four floors at the sight of the doctor. It had to be all those years of watching juries come back into the courtroom to deliver a verdict.

"Well, ladies, I'm happy to give you good news. Initially, I told you we were probably looking at stage 2 cancer. But now that we've done the surgery and had the chance to look at the tumor, it turns out that it is only at stage one."

"And my lymph nodes?"

The surgeon smiled. "More good news. They were clear. No sign that the cancer has spread."

Beth nodded her head and continued with her questions, as if checking them off a list in her head. "Do you have the results of the BRCA genetic test?"

"You don't have the gene."

Beth shut her eyes, took another deep breath, and nodded her head as she digested the information. It was the first bit of emotion she'd revealed since arriving at the doctor's office that morning.

Beth set aside her relief and moved on to the next question. "What about chemotherapy?"

The surgeon leaned forward. "That isn't my call. It is going to be up to your oncologist. But I think you have a good chance of skipping chemotherapy because the genetic testing results on your tumor look really good so far."

"What does that mean?"

"It is slow growing. It isn't aggressive. Your tumor's characteristics will factor into the final decision on radiation or chemotherapy. But again, it isn't up to me. Your oncologist and a panel of doctors will review your medical file and make the final recommendation. They will weigh whether the benefits of those treatments outweigh the toll they take on the body."

"So, just to make sure that I'm hearing you correctly, you're saying that my tumor is rather lazy so there is a chance that I could skip chemo and move forward with the breast reconstruction phase?"

"Again, I can't make you any promises," the surgeon cautioned. "But you are a candidate for this newer, more conservative treatment. In the last few years, we've stopped taking the fire hose approach to cancer. We recognize that radiation and chemotherapy, while extremely helpful, also have harmful side effects. In some cases, the harm of the treatment doesn't outweigh the benefit."

"I won't get my hopes up," Beth said even as her lips formed a smile.

It was just before noon when Debbie entered Sam's office.

"How'd your mom's appointment go?" Sam asked without looking up from the proofs he was reviewing. He edited stories on his desktop. But for the final proofing, he was old-fashioned. He preferred paper.

Debbie sat down on the edge of the chair across from her editor's desk. "Better than we could have ever hoped for. Turns out she had stage one cancer. She may not even need chemo."

"Hmmm. I didn't know they did that," Sam said as he set aside the paper marked with red-pen hieroglyphics and looked at the reporter.

"One of the advantages of being treated at a leading cancer hospital, I guess," Debbie said. "They even test the genetic makeup of the tumor, to customize the treatment."

Sam studied Debbie carefully. "Could make a good story. Our readers would be interested. The cancer center would be grateful for the publicity. So, does the good news mean you'll be trying to get your old job back in D.C.?"

"Honestly, I hadn't even thought of that," Debbie lied. "I've just been focused on my mom and trying to get myself reestablished here."

"There's a lot more action in D.C. than there is in the heartland," Sam remarked.

"That's true. But I don't know that I'm ready to deal with," Debbie paused, "some issues that I left unresolved in D.C. Besides, everything that the doctor said about my mom today was predicated with caveats and don't-get-your-hopes-up-too-high language."

"Well, I'm just saying that it would be a pity to lose you now," Sam said. "Crime Beat Girl is gaining traction. Lots of social media shares. Even your less-than-professional photos are getting some notice on Instagram. Our owner is very happy. He's already pushing for more video; says it will increase time-on-page. He wants you to add the Crime Beat Girl moniker to your social media accounts. And he's even considering building a podcast room."

"No pressure, huh? Try to slow him down a bit," Debbie pleaded. "I know these tech guys are push, push, push, but I haven't even gotten business cards. And I should have never agreed to that name. You may force me to leave St. Louis to get rid of it," Debbie said. "That reminds me, I need to do some last-minute fact checking on the Jarrett story. Make sure I've got all the names and dates right. Instead of calling, I think I'm going to drop by his grandmother's house, if she's cool with it."

"What else are you working on?"

"Don't I get a breather?" Debbie answered. "I'm working on nothing and everything."

"That's not going to feed the monster," Sam said pointedly, referring to the constant need for content.

"I know. I have a lot of questions, but no answers. I have one defendant in the Travis Hunt murder, but the other people involved haven't been identified. There's the shooting outside the abandoned building. No one's been arrested. And how is it that the same gun was used in both murders? Was Roberto Simmons involved in both? I'm also keeping an eye on the grocery store carjacking."

"I've been looking at the crime stats," Sam said. "If we keep up this pace of violence, it is going to be one of the bloodiest summers on record in St. Louis; maybe that's your next story."

"Aren't the civic leaders, many of whom are our readers, going to object to that sort of piece?" Debbie asked.

"Of course. But we can start it by noting that stats are misleading because they don't include the whole metro area. I actually agree with the St. Louis cheerleaders on that point. It is unfair to judge our area without including the suburbs. Anyway, let me worry about that. You know, we could create a collage of the murder victims so far this year—put faces on the numbers. Each of the names could be clickable. When you click, you get the biographical information of the victim, the place of the crime, whether anyone has been charged in the killing. And we could have an interactive map with the location of each murder."

"That's going to be a lot of work," Debbie said as she felt her phone vibrate. She checked the screen. "City government number. Could be the police department. I should probably get it," Debbie said before answering, "Debbie Bradley."

"Ms. Bradley, Detective Flannery."

"So nice of you to call, Detective Flannery," Debbie said for her boss to hear. "What can I do for you?"

"Seems the mayor was miffed about the fact that you made me look like a good guy. So now guess who wants to meet with you?"

"Who? The mayor?" Debbie asked.

"Yes, the mayor," Flannery replied. "I guess they've noticed that your obscure column isn't so obscure anymore. I heard some of his big campaign donors are calling to compliment him on my work," the detective said, unable to suppress a chuckle.

"How do you know this?"

"The mayor calls the police chief. The police chief calls me," Flannery said. "Anyway, I'm just giving you a heads-up. The mayor's office isn't going to call you and ask for an interview. What they want is for you to call and ask them. This is all ridiculous, but it seems that I've been nominated to be the guy who floats the test balloon, as I guess PR people call it. I don't know why they gave the task to me, other than I've had the most contact with you. As you can see, I'm rather blunt and I don't have time for these stupid PR games."

"Um, okay," Debbie said. "I'll give the mayor's PR flack a call in just a bit. Thanks for passing along the information. Anything else?"

"Nope, that is it," Flannery said. "I'm sure we'll run into each other at another crime scene. You are, after all, Crime Beat Girl," he said. Debbie could hear him chuckle as he hung up the phone.

Just as the call disconnected, Debbie's phone vibrated again. She looked down and then decided to answer. "Hello?"

"Debbie, this is Chase Laclede," the voice on the line began.

"Chase," Debbie said. Her editor's eyebrows rose. "How are you?"

"You suggested lunch the other day. Is the invite still open?"

"Absolutely. When do you want to get together?"

"I've got court in the morning. I never know exactly when it'll end. Could be early. Could be late. How about dinner tonight?"

"Dinner? Tonight?" Debbie repeated. Sam smiled. "Um, sure. But you name the place and time. Just text me the details this afternoon and I'll be there."

Debbie hung up and looked at Sam.

"Would be a real shame for you to leave St. Louis now," her editor said.

A sleeveless turquoise summer dress with a narrow waist and a slim skirt that hit just above the knee, paired with white sandals, was the outfit Debbie chose for her dinner meeting with Chase. Not too formal, not too casual. Confident but relaxed. Attractive, but not too sexy. She'd spent twenty minutes staring at her limited wardrobe wondering whether male journalists wasted as much time pondering their appearance, and the unintended signals they could be sending, before key meetings. But after living with Christian, she already knew the answer: No.

Chase had suggested meeting on South Grand, an area of the city known for a cluster of restaurants serving a variety of international fare. He picked a well-established place that had branded its Iranian roots as Persian cuisine.

Debbie arrived a few minutes before the agreed hour. Chase was already there, seated at a table next to a window that looked out onto the busy street.

"You're on time," Chase said as he stood up.

"You're early," Debbie replied as she pulled out the chair across from her dinner companion and sat down.

Chase was wearing a white polo shirt and dark-blue slim-fit pants. His Sperrys rounded out the affluent, prep school look.

"I took the liberty of ordering a pomegranate yogurt appetizer with pita bread. I hope you don't mind," Chase said. "I came straight from the office. I'm starving."

Debbie smiled. "No problem. Never tried it. What were you working on, Joshua's case? Or Roberto Simmons's?"

"Slow down," Chase said as he sat down. "Catch your breath. I'm not running away. You don't have to try shoot rapid-fire questions at me in the hopes of getting a few answers before I bolt. To be honest, I'm simply too hungry to leave."

Debbie inhaled, set her hands on her lap, and concentrated on relaxing her shoulders as she let out her breath. "Let's start over. You know, when I was a kid, it used to drive me crazy when my parents would come home but stay stuck in lawyer mode. I can't tell you how many times I was cross-examined—especially when I was a teenager. Now, I seem to follow in their footsteps. I bring my work persona into my private life. I guess I have a tough time of letting go of my reporter instincts, even in a casual setting."

The waitress appeared with the appetizer.

Chase nodded. "I had the same issues with my parents. I get it. And my personal identity is, unfortunately, tightly wound up in my professional work as a lawyer. My mom keeps telling me that it isn't healthy. That I need to work harder to be more than Chase 'The Lawyer.'"

Debbie took a piece of bread, dipped it in the pomegranate yogurt appetizer, and took a bite. "Wow, this is good." She placed the food on the appetizer plate in front of her and then held up her hands. "Look, no notebook. No pen. No tape recorder. Nothing is on the record."

"Good, I wanted this to be a friendly dinner," Chase replied.

Debbie wiped her hands on her burgundy napkin. "That said, I am genuinely curious as to why you work so hard. Especially on the criminal defense side. I mean, I can understand Joshua Lucas. He's just a kid. There are, one could argue, mitigating circumstances. He could have found the car and just been unable to resist an abandoned red Audi with the keys in the ignition. But Roberto Simmons? And how in the heck can his family afford you?"

Chase smiled. "What you're really asking me is how I can represent people I believe are guilty of committing a crime, right?"

"No, not exactly," Debbie answered. "Well. Maybe."

"Let me see if I can explain," he began. "And let me preface this by saying that I don't have any idea whether Roberto Simmons committed the acts that the state accuses him of. In fact, I learned something earlier today that may very well get the charges dropped. But more on that later. And off the record."

He sipped his tea and then leaned forward. "First, I believe in the Constitution. Because you're a reporter, you must believe in it too. I have sworn an oath to protect and defend the Constitution. I also believe in the adversarial criminal justice system. Finally, I believe it is better to let ten guilty men go free than convict one innocent man. Because those are part of my core principles, I don't question the constitutional right to a fair trial. A defendant doesn't get the benefit of that right if I think my job is to put my client on trial in the office before they enter the courtroom. No. As a defense lawyer, my job is to represent the defendant as best I can so long as I follow the ethical rules and stay within the law. That means I can't put my client on the stand and let my client tell a lie—if I know he's lying. I can't help my client commit future crimes. But I can make sure that the rules are followed and that the process is fair. The prosecutor, the judge, the jury are the ones responsible for convictions, not me."

Debbie sat back in her chair. "You don't think that putting a bad guy behind bars is a good reason to skirt the legal processes, cut constitutional corners?"

Chase shook his head emphatically. "The Bill of Rights protects all Americans from unreasonable searches and seizures. We all have the right to remain silent. And every person is innocent until proven guilty—not guilty until proven innocent. Constitutional rights apply to all, not just the people who are rich, or who look like us, or who act like us, or who worship like us. And besides, I've seen too many well-meaning people do bad things because they believed that the end justified the means."

"Perhaps," Debbie said.

"We're not so different, Debbie Bradley. Let me put it this way. Let's say you support a scrappy politician who supports gay marriage, reasonable gun laws, and health care for all, liberal causes that I'm guessing you favor. But let's say you find out through your work that the same politician has an unseemly side, that he or she broke campaign finance laws or was accepting bribes. Would you sit on the story to ensure that health care and gay marriage are preserved? Or would you report about it?"

"No brainer. I'd report it," Debbie said.

"And why is that?"

"Because I'm a journalist, not an advocate. My duty is to the truth and to the reader. I guess, as you say, the end doesn't justify the means."

"Now you see my position," Chase said. "I may not always agree with my clients, but I agree with our Constitution. That is the oath I've taken, and it is the oath I will honor. And I owe a duty to my client. But my allegiance isn't just to the client, it is to the Constitution and the law."

The waitress reappeared.

"I haven't had a chance to look at the menu yet," Debbie said. "What do you recommend?" she asked Chase.

"How do you feel about lamb?" he asked.

"Too heavy," Debbie replied.

"Vegetarian or meat?"

"I guess you could say I'm a flexitarian."

"The chicken koobideh is good. It is a mix of ground chicken, saffron, and turmeric," he recommended. "Along with the side of saffron rice."

"Okay, give me that."

"I'm hungry. I'll have the ghormeh sabzi," Chase informed the waitress. "Lamb may not be the healthiest, but this stew with parsley and cilantro is amazing," Chase admitted. "Besides, I'll compensate for my meal this next week with a vegetarian diet and plenty of visits to the gym."

"How did you become such an expert on Middle Eastern cuisine?" Debbie asked.

Chase smiled. "I have to admit that I am, to use the slang of teenagers, extra."

"Extra?"

"Over the top. Pampered. Spoiled," Chase said. "My parents have given me every opportunity imaginable. I spent a semester of college studying in Spain. In addition to touring Europe, I spent some time in Morocco and Turkey. Every place I go, I try to immerse myself in the culture. One of the best ways to get to know a place is through food—and I love trying new things."

"So, you've traveled around the world. You've lived abroad. You're clearly smart and talented. And yet, you came back to St. Louis," Debbie observed. "Why?"

"I guess I could run down the list of the usual advantages that people cite to justify living here. The cost of living is reasonable, compared to the coasts. It was easier for me to start a law practice where I had some roots, and quite frankly, connections."

"But those are the easy reasons," Debbie replied. "What was the real reason you returned home after experiencing so much of the world outside of St. Louis?"

Chase pointed to the busy sidewalk on the other side of the window. A middle-aged white couple passed a twenty-something woman with purple-tinged hair clad in black and sporting a nose piercing and tattoos. A young African-American family pushed a stroller. An immigrant woman in a burka carrying a grocery bag from the international grocery store on the street corner hustled down the sidewalk with two small children trailing behind her.

"We can look out the window here onto South Grand and see diversity. But it is a pocket in St. Louis. There's still a lot of economic and racial segregation. And that was even before Ferguson. As a child of a black father and a white mother, I've experienced the good and the bad this town has to offer. Maybe I loved St. Louis more after I had a chance to leave. I wanted to come back home and use my talents to make this a better place—for all."

Chase paused. "And what about you? You chose to leave. And come back. Do you miss D.C.?"

Christian's image popped into Debbie's mind. She winced.

"Sensitive subject?" Chase asked.

"No," Debbie said.

"No to missing D.C. or no to the question of being sensitive?"

"Um, I plan to go back. I hope to go back. Unlike lawyers, reporters have a short shelf life, especially in this era of dying newspapers. Lawyers are just hitting their stride by the time they reach forty. But when reporters reach that age, they're over the hill. And now it seems my mother is doing better. There are a few more tests that have to be done, but if she doesn't need chemo or radiation, then I might try to get my old job back."

"It'd be a shame for you leave town," Chase said. "You seem to be doing well here. After all, I swore that I'd never trust a journalist. Yet I'm having dinner with one."

"I don't know if I'm doing well," Debbie admitted. "I've been in the right place at the right time. Or, more accurately, the wrong place at the right time. But now I feel like I've hit a dead end."

"Well, as I mentioned earlier, and this is completely off the record, I learned something earlier today that you'll find interesting."

Chase paused and looked at her. Debbie could sense he was having second thoughts about telling her what he'd learned.

"You have my promise," Debbie said. "Off the record."

"So, you remember the carjacking at the grocery store?"

"How can I forget it?"

"I have a source who has an inside track to the SLMPD's crime lab. The cops found the bullet that they believe was shot at the mom. Seems it hit a nearby car."

"Yes?"

"The cops rushed an analysis of it."

"Interesting. So what'd they find?"

"Well, this isn't official yet. But what I'm hearing is that the bullet matches the bullets that killed Travis Hunt."

Debbie took the bit of information in and pondered it for a moment. "But Roberto Simmons is in jail, was in jail at the time of the carjacking. And he's black. The suspects in the carjacking are white."

"I know."

The waitress, carrying plates of food, interrupted as she set down their meals.

"Are you one hundred percent sure on this?"

"No," Chase admitted. "I only have the hearsay of my source. However, I'll be filing a Brady motion asking for the test results," Chase said, referring to the case that requires prosecutors to turn over exculpatory evidence when asked by the defense.

"That's the one. If the lab report confirms what I've heard, then I'm going to move to dismiss the charges against my client. I'll argue that there's no way Roberto Simmons could be mistaken for one of the two white guys involved in the carjacking."

Debbie picked up her fork. "You know I'm regretting the off-the-record promise, don't you?"

Chase smiled. "Of course. I'd be shocked if you didn't want to break your promise. But you won't. I'm guessing you'll find a way to keep your promise to me and track down an independent source who can back this up. You just have to work harder and wait a bit longer."

"Hard work, I don't mind," Debbie said as she picked up her fork. "Waiting? That's never been a strength of mine."

13 SNITCHES

The house was built with red St. Louis brick. The window frames and cornices were painted the color of dark summer leaves that some called South City green—even though the shade was popular on the North Side, too. Hot pink geranium blooms cascaded out of orange clay pots perched on the edge of each brick step that led up to the front porch.

When Debbie called Ada Davis before her dinner with Chase and asked to stop by the next morning, Ada hesitated, fearing her home wasn't clean enough for visitors. Debbie got the grandmother to change her mind by appealing to Ada's unspoken concern that some tidbit in the story about her family would be wrong.

Before Debbie could finish climbing the porch stairs, the front door swung open.

"I heard you pull up. I was keeping an eye out. You can never be too careful," Ada said as she ushered Debbie into the home, which smelled of lemon furniture polish, Murphy's wood oil soap, and bacon. "I was just making some breakfast for Jarrett. He stayed the night so his parents could have a bit of a break. They've been working so much that they haven't had time to be together as a couple. Why don't you come on back? You look like you could use some food."

Debbie smiled. It was true, all she'd had that morning was a cup of coffee.

"Hey, Jarrett," Debbie said as she walked into the kitchen. The young man, clad in a red T-shirt and gray sweatpants, was slumped over the kitchen table, marking up a workbook with the pen in his hand.

Ada tapped on him on the shoulder. "Sit up and mind your manners."

"Sorry," he said sheepishly. "I was up late."

"Having fun? Playing video games?" Debbie asked.

He shook his head. "Naw. Studying. For the ACT. Miss Darlinda gave me some books with practice tests. I need a scholarship."

"Your books bring back memories, Jarrett. I studied for the college entrance exam, too," Debbie said, though she didn't add that her parents also sent her to an expensive ACT prep class. She'd complained bitterly about having to take it. But now, seeing Jarrett, Debbie felt guilty about the advantages she'd taken for granted.

"You know, if you take it and don't like the score, you can always retake it," Debbie noted.

"Yeah," Jarrett said with a sigh. "But then my parents may have to pay more money."

"True," Debbie admitted.

"Sit," Ada commanded as she put a plate of scrambled eggs, bacon, and toast in front of Debbie. "Coffee?"

"Please," Debbie said as she pulled out a chair to sit at a table covered with a blue and white checked cloth. "Just straight, no cream or sugar."

Debbie reached into her oversized purse that doubled as a backpack and briefcase and pulled out a manila folder. "I typed up some notes last night; things I wanted to double check with you. Unfortunately, I can't bring the draft of the story for you to review. It wouldn't be proper journalism. But I can tell you that the story is a positive one."

"Aw. You're not going to let me take a peek at it?" Jarrett asked. "I won't tell," he added, a conspiratorial smile turning his lips.

"Now Jarrett," Ada admonished. "You heard her say that's not proper." Turning to Debbie, Ada urged, "Why don't you go on and ask your questions."

The list was straightforward. Debbie started off with the spelling of the names of family members. She'd learned the hard way that people don't forgive—or forget—when you botch their names. After checking names, Debbie verified important dates and names of places.

"That's it?" Jarrett asked when Debbie was done.

"Yep, that's it. It may not seem like much, but every little mistake undermines my credibility. And it is so easy to screw up. You know, the night before something big I write gets published, like a profile or an investigative article, I can't sleep. My brain goes over the story again and again to make sure that I triple checked everything."

"Kinda like after I take a final," Jarrett said. "I can't stop going over my answers in my head. But you wouldn't feel so anxious if you just let me peek at it."

"Nice try," Debbie said. "I applaud your persistence. It is an underappreciated quality that will take you far. How about a compromise? I can show you the photos that I think are going to run with the piece. I've got them in a Dropbox folder on my phone. Do you want a sneak peek?"

"Oh yeah!" Jarrett's head nodded vigorously.

Debbie punched in her extra pass code for the app.

"You're using different passwords for all your accounts, right?" Jarrett asked.

"Of course. And two-factor authentication for sign-in. Journalists can't be too careful. I even have a special encrypted email service. I started using it as a reporter in D.C."

"Excellent," Jarrett said.

"Okay, here are the pictures. You can just scroll through," Debbie said as she handed Jarrett her phone, trusting him with a device that was the gateway to many of her secrets.

Ada and Jarrett huddled together. With each swipe, Ada smiled. When she saw the photo of her sitting next to her grandson at the Teen Alliance fundraiser, she laughed.

"How proud my husband is right now," was all she said.

Jarrett said nothing, but Debbie could feel the weight of the expectations that he carried on his young shoulders.

"You know, Jarrett, I'm really hoping this will help your quest for a scholarship," Debbie volunteered.

Jarrett nodded. "Thank you, Miss Debbie. I don't want to let anybody down. Gran, do you need help with the dishes?" he asked.

She smiled. "You just go on back to the living room. Keep studyin'."

"I'd be glad to help," Debbie volunteered.

"You're a guest. Guests don't do dishes."

"Seems like a small price to pay for a delicious breakfast. I didn't realize I was so hungry. Even after eating dinner last night with Chase Laclede."

Ada paused as she picked the plates off the table. "Ladies never eat much when they're on a date."

Debbie blushed. "It was just work. I swear."

"Mmmhmm," Ada replied. "He's a handsome young man. I wouldn't blame you. So what were you working on, if it wasn't a date?"

"I have a lot of stories that I'm interested in, but they're not ripe. I'm stuck," Debbie admitted.

"Why is that? Can't you just write?" Ada asked.

Debbie shook her head. "I wish it were that easy. I've got a lot of open questions right now."

"What kinda questions?" Ada asked as she poured Debbie another cup of coffee, sensing her guest was ready for a refill.

"I've got three crimes I'm tracking. They happened in different parts of the city. I don't think they're related. And yet, I have a good reason to believe the same gun was used in all of them. I just can't figure out the connection."

"For someone so smart, you don't know much about how things work in the real world, do you?" Ada said as she sat down.

"What do you mean?" Debbie asked.

"Look, you know how you can go to the library and check out a book?" Ada asked.

"Sure, of course," Debbie answered.

"On the street, instead of books, some people check out guns," Ada said.

"What?"

"Mmmhmmm," Ada replied. "You got all types who want to get their hands on guns. Kids who are too

146

young or too poor. Grown-ups with records. And there are so many guns floating around town. And people who can legally get guns sometimes get them stolen. I wouldn't be surprised if you got a pistol in that purse of yours, given the neighborhoods you're heading into alone."

Debbie opened her bag for Ada. "Nope. I don't think I'd have the nerve to shoot. Then the gun would just be used against me. Besides, the keyboard is mightier than the firearm."

"I wouldn't be too sure about that," Ada said. "But look, if you're a kid or a criminal, you can't be caught with a gun. So instead, guns are like those scooters I see fools out on the streets ridin'. People don't own the scooters, they just rent 'em. In many a neighborhood, there's spots where you can find a gun tucked away. People just borrow it and put it back. Gettin' ammo is easy. But gettin' a gun can be harder."

"A lethal library? But why don't people who live in the neighborhoods tell the police?"

Ada pointed to the next room, where Jarrett had resumed his studies. "That's why. We live here. Contrary to what outsiders think, there are lots of hardworking, law-abiding folks just trying to get through each day. People who love their families. And they don't want to see them get hurt. They keep their heads down and mind their own business."

Ada sat back in her chair. "Bad things can happen to snitches. Bad things can happen to the families of snitches. And the police aren't always your friends. Too much history with the law in these neighborhoods. What's crazy is that my son, Jarrett's uncle, is a cop. And I'm proud of him. But even having a police officer in the family doesn't stop run-ins. Jarrett's dad has been stopped many times while minding his own business. Even Jarrett has been stopped while walking on the sidewalk, forced to answer questions from the police."

Debbie frowned. "But Jarrett is a good kid."

"Yes, he is. But you gotta make it through each day."

Ada continued, "I try to be a good neighbor, even with the broken families, the ones struggling with drugs and dysfunction. I bake cookies for the kids. A baby today is a teenager tomorrow. I try to make sure they always have a soft spot for my treats."

"I see. You win people through their stomachs. Like you did with me."

Ada smiled. "I know the Good Lord says pride is a sin. But I can't help it. I'm proud of my cooking. Oh, that reminds me. I have cornbread for your mother. I heard she's sick. And I've got a huge batch for sharin'."

Debbie stopped. "How'd you know?"

"I told you that my son is on the police force. He asked around about you. Told me about your parents. I thought your mom could use something. I know what it's like to be facing hard stuff without your husband. Even if you've got kids. It just isn't the same as having your man."

Debbie nodded as she stood up. "I suppose I really hadn't thought of it that way."

"Of course you didn't," Ada said with a smile. "Most kids don't."

Slinging her purse over her arm and picking up the plastic container filled with cornbread, Debbie said, "I guess it's time for me to get going. Thank you for everything. I know that my mom will appreciate these. As do I, because you know I won't be able to resist them. I'll be sure to return your container."

"It was the least I could do," she said, flicking her hands as though she was whisking away Debbie's words and walking toward the front door. "Oh, and don't worry about the plastic. I have a cupboard full of them. I give food away and food seems to come back to me. I seem to have a never-ending supply of Rubbermaid containers and Ziploc freezer bags. I was a recycler before it was trendy."

Debbie looked at Jarrett as she passed the living room on her way to the front door. "Good luck with your studies today."

Jarrett looked away from the workbook he'd been scribbling in. "Thanks, Miss Debbie."

Ada opened the door for Debbie and stepped out on the porch. "I know you're a grown woman. But I always make sure my visitors make it out safely."

"I appreciate it," Debbie said as she descended the steps. Ada's home had a comforting warmth that left Debbie glowing inside. She reached her car then turned to wave goodbye. A single shot rang out. A metallic ping made Debbie bounce as a bullet ricocheted off her car. Debbie ducked her head. She dropped the container of cornbread in her hands, the contents spilling out onto the street.

The noise ended as abruptly as it began. Debbie looked at Ada, who stood frozen in the doorway.

"Your hand!" Ada shouted. Then, like a medic on a battlefield, Ada commanded: "Jarrett, call 911!"

A paramedic was wrapping a bandage around Debbie's hand when Flannery arrived.

A bullet had pierced the driver's side window of Debbie's car, leaving a hole with fracture lines spreading out from the center. A small shard of glass had hit her hand. As Jarrett dialed emergency, Ada had rushed out with a towel to put pressure on Debbie's wound.

The ambulance arrived about ten minutes after Ada worked to stop the bleeding. Flannery wasn't far behind.

"What are you doing here?" Debbie asked.

"I'm a cop. There was a shooting."

"I'm not surprised to see a cop. I'm surprised to see you."

"I think Jarrett called his uncle," Flannery said.

"The police officer?"

"Yep. His uncle knew I kept having run-ins with you; thought I'd want to know."

Debbie rubbed the bandage and flexed her fingers to make sure the wrapping wasn't too tight.

"The side windows aren't as strong as the windshield glass. Someone was either very deliberate with their aim or they got lucky. What were you doing here anyway?"

"I had stopped by to fact check the story about Jarrett and Teen Alliance. I was just leaving."

"Did you see anyone when you walked outside?"

"Besides Mrs. Davis?" Debbie said. "No."

Flannery asked, "Mind if I search your car?"

"Knock yourself out."

The driver's side door was already open. Debbie had left it ajar when she was struck by the glass.

"It appears that the bullet entered from the outside," Flannery said, stating the obvious, as if he was already drafting the narrative of his police report. He walked around the vehicle and opened the passenger door. "Here!" he said, pointing to a deformed bullet that lay on the floor. "We'll have to have the crime lab test it, but I guess that the shooter was pretty far away because the bullet didn't get too far. It looks like it was deflected down."

He summoned one of the officers getting out of a crime lab van who began taking photos and gathering evidence.

"Look," he said to Debbie after directing the evidence technician, "your car is going to need to be towed. There's shattered glass all over the front seat. I know a mechanic who'll fix it—and he won't overcharge you. Do you want to have the tow truck take your car there after we get done here?"

Debbie nodded. "Yeah. I talked to my insurance agent already. I've got to pay a five-hundred-dollar deductible. We'll see how much it costs to get the window replaced."

"Do you need a lift somewhere?" Flannery asked.

"Naw, I'll just go with the tow truck driver. And I'll ask my mom to pick me up from the repair shop."

Flannery reached out one hand. "Here, hand me your reporter's notebook."

Debbie eyed him suspiciously. He may as well have just asked for her diary, already opened to the page with the juiciest tidbits.

"I just want to write down the name of a good mechanic," Flannery said.

"Oh," Debbie muttered as she flipped to a blank page and handed the notebook to him. He scribbled a name and address and handed it back to her.

"My guy won't take advantage of you. Just show it to the tow truck driver and tell him Detective Flannery recommended the place."

The tow truck driver who climbed into the cab next to Debbie smelled of sweat and grease. There was a smudge of oil on his forearm. He wiped his hands with a dirty pink rag before starting the engine and grabbing the wheel with his thick fingers.

"Where to?" he asked gruffly. "If you need a rec, I know some good mechanics."

Debbie flipped open her reporter's notebook and read the name Flannery had given her.

He frowned. "I know it. They do good work. A favorite of cops and folks who don't like to be ripped off."

Attempting to make small talk, Debbie asked, "So, how long have you been driving a tow truck?"

"Forever," the man replied as he removed some chewing tobacco from a pouch and put a pinch below his lower lip.

For Debbie, it was hard to judge what would qualify as forever for this man. The grime from his dirty job made it hard to see the clues that might reveal his age. His hair was an oily blond that needed a shampoo. If there was any gray, she couldn't see it. Even though his hair was thin, it could've been its natural state rather than anything related to aging. Because he worked outside, his face was weathered and tan, which could make it look like he'd spent longer on the earth than he actually had.

"What are the easiest jobs that you do when you're called to tow a car?" Debbie asked.

The man sniffed, wiped his nose with the back of his hand, and replied, "That's simple. People like you. Though I don't know what a gal like you was doing in a neighborhood like this. Ain't safe," he said as he picked up an empty cup to spit tobacco juice into.

"Why do you say I was an easy job?" she asked.

"You sure ask a lot of questions, so maybe I'm going to change my answer," he said.

"I'm just curious. Just making conversation. You must encounter all sorts of people every day. I was wondering what made me so easy."

"You're still alive," he said. "That makes you easy."

"Then the hard ones..." Debbie began before she was interrupted.

"The hard ones are the dead ones. When you gotta hook up a car, and someone's guts are still inside. Well, that ain't easy."

The driver picked up his cup and brown spit came out again.

Twenty-four hours with a tow truck driver, Debbie thought. Could be a story pitch. She doubted that Sam would go for it, but then again, at least it was something she could throw out as an idea.

"Say, you didn't happen to work an accident a few weeks ago where a boy stole a red Audi and ended up hitting and killing a girl, did you?"

The driver nodded. "Yeah, I was there. Teenagers bunched together. Easy target for a street rat who had no business being behind the wheel."

"That one went to Ace Towing, right?" Debbie said.

"Yep," the driver answered.

"But I didn't see an Ace Towing logo on your truck."

"No one owns me. I'm an entrepreneur," he said proudly. "I got my truck and arrangements with companies all over town. They call me when they don't have enough manpower. The big tow truck companies— the ones with big lots—they got all the best city contracts locked up. Even if I had a lot, I'd still need someone on the inside to help me win a city contract. I don't have any connections. I just have my muscle, my smarts, and a reputation for being reliable. And it keeps me plenty busy. In fact, lately, it seems like I'm picking up a stolo a day."

Debbie had second thoughts about calling her mother for a ride. Instead, she resorted to a Lyft. And when she got home, she found Beth seated at the kitchen table in front of an open laptop, a container of cornbread on the cabinet next to her.

"Where'd you get that?" Debbie asked, recognizing Ada's handiwork. The original batch Debbie had received spilled on the street. This had to be a substitute offering.

"Detective Flannery," Beth answered.

"Flannery? He was here?"

"Mmmhmmm," Beth answered, sipping from a cup of tea. Turmeric, Debbie guessed from the scent.

"So, he told you about the car?"

"He told me about the shooting, if that's what you mean," Beth said. "And he somehow sensed that you weren't going to call me—even though you told him you would."

"I was going to tell you. I just didn't want to bother you. I know you're still recuperating. And you've got work to do."

"I could've still gotten in my car to get you. I'm allowed behind the wheel now. All I can say is thank goodness for Detective Flannery—and Mrs. Davis. At least they figured I'd want to know. And I think they guessed you wouldn't tell me, or tell me much. I think the cornbread was just an excuse to feed me info."

"Geez, Mom, I'm an adult. I was gonna tell you. I did live in D.C. I encountered way more dangerous situations there than I have here. And you didn't worry."

"But that's just it. I didn't know about it. When you're away, I don't worry. But as long as we're living together, I worry more. Old habits die hard. I can't help it."

"Well, as you can see, I'm fine."

"Your hand doesn't look fine."

"It's fine," Debbie said, reflexively hiding it behind her back as if that would somehow prevent her mother from focusing on the injury. "It's just a cut. No stitches. Just some glass."

Debbie placed a tea bag into a coffee cup and poured hot water from an electric kettle into it.

"And my car just needs a new window. Unfortunately, my deductible is high, so I've gotta pay out of pocket."

"You need a loan?"

Debbie sat down and wrapped her hands around the mug. Even though it was warm outside, the heat on her palms was comforting.

"I hate relying on the Bank of Mom," Debbie said.

"I know. And I don't want you to rely on me. But I know money's tight for you, at least temporarily. And we should sit down at some point and talk about money management strategies. I think every woman should know how to use a hammer and how to save and invest. Your dad wasn't so good at finances. I was always the one who put together budgets for our household and our law practice. I took care of the cash flow and made sure there was always enough for a rainy day. For lawyers, it can be feast or famine. And when you've got employees counting on you, the first person who goes without a paycheck is the one whose name is on the door."

"Mom, the last thing I want is a money lecture," Debbie said.

"I'm not lecturing. Really. And I'm not judging. I was young once. I know what it's like starting out; struggling to establish your career and build a solid financial base. I feel a lot of empathy for you. I just want to share some tools to help you. Tools that you'll need to manage your estate you'll inherit once I'm gone."

"Don't say that, please."

"It is going to happen someday."

"What? Did you get some news today about the cancer?"

"No. Everything is the same as it was. But all of this has made me consider revisiting my estate planning. I'd like to have you more involved in the process. I want to sit down with a trust and estates lawyer and go over our options. If I create a trust, you would end up being a trustee someday."

Debbie let out a sigh.

"I don't know how we got on this, but I'm worn out. Yes, we can talk about estate planning. But not now, okay?"

"Fair enough," Beth said. "By the way, if you're hungry, I highly recommend the cornbread."

"I know, right? Ada's a good cook. I ate breakfast over there this morning. I'm surprised she gave Flannery the job of delivering baked goods to you, though. She's got a son who's a cop."

Beth sipped her tea. "Perhaps she trusts Flannery. And, after all, he was at her house so it was convenient. There's something, some quality about him, that encourages trust. He's, um, solid."

"Solid?"

"Dependable. Reliable. At least that was my impression. You know as well as I do how rare it is find those traits in people. Someone who isn't a flake, overly dramatic, or a complete narcissist. You know, he may not tell you all the secrets you want to hear, but that doesn't make him a bad guy. And I'll tell you this: Denise Robertson is an idiot. I'd pick Flannery over our weak-chinned mayor any day."

"So I take it you liked Flannery?" Debbie teased.

Beth waved her hand. "Oh stop."

"Amazing. I'd rather talk about Flannery than discuss handling your money when you're gone. You spend too much time worrying about everyone else—me, your clients. Have you considered that maybe you've been given a second chance? A wakeup call? I know you loved Dad, that you still love him. But I don't think Dad would want you to get up every day, go to work, come home, worry about me, then start all over again. I think he'd want you to enjoy life more, worry less."

Beth closed her laptop and got off from the table to pour more hot water in her mug. "It's hard not to worry when someone is shooting at your daughter."

"We don't know if I was the target. And besides, the tow truck driver said I was an easy call."

"What'd he mean?"

"He just said that he'd seen much worse than my vehicle," Debbie answered. "He was an odd duck. But interesting. Although he seemed disappointed when I gave him the name of the mechanic that Flannery recommended."

Beth's brow furrowed. "You might've cost him some money."

"What do you mean?"

"Perhaps the mechanic Flannery sent you to is an honest one who doesn't give a kickback to tow truck drivers," Beth said.

Debbie shook her head. "No matter where I turn lately, there's some undercurrent that I'm missing," she said. "I'm beginning to think I'm losing my keen perceptive abilities."

"When you're in the midst of a crisis, as you were today, it's hard to see things clearly. Plus, you're losing your detachment as you become part of the story, Crime Beat Girl."

Debbie frowned. "Well, I need my superpowers back fast. It looks like I've got an interview with the mayor tomorrow."

14 UNDER THE BUS

As Debbie walked into city hall, she recalled how much her father had admired the building.

Constructed over the course of several years starting in the late 1800s and into the early 1900s, the French Renaissance Revival style of the structure was meant to pay homage to the city's roots. The red tile roof, the yellow stone set upon rose-colored stone, had always fascinated her dad. And the father's enthusiasm for the building had been transferred to his daughter. Only for Debbie, it was the giant clock on the outside that she found most intriguing.

"You know where you're going?"

A sheriff's deputy interrupted Debbie's reverie as she cleared the metal detector and collected her purse from the scanner.

"Mayor's office," Debbie answered.

"Room 200. Elevator's around the corner."

Debbie made a beeline for the grand staircase. Moments later, she had walked through the outer set of double doors, the first threshold that had to be crossed to see the man who had summoned her. His public relations chief, a woman dressed in a tailored navy pantsuit, looked at her smartphone and said, "Debbie Bradley, I presume. You're punctual. Mayor Robertson is ready for you. Why don't we head on into his office?"

With no time for pleasantries, Debbie obeyed. The flack led the way, then dissolved into a corner of the large office as Robertson crossed the burgundy wall-to-wall carpet, skirting around the common seal of St. Louis, a riverboat in the center of the image, that had been embedded into the fabric of the rug.

The mayor was maybe six feet tall, Debbie guessed as she shook his hand. His bright blue eyes complemented his ash blond hair. And while his chin wasn't as chiseled as Flannery's, Debbie wouldn't describe it as weak. Like his press aide, Mayor Robertson wore a navy suit. However, his uniform was offset by a crisp white shirt and a burgundy tie that matched the carpet. In his lapel, a pin with the city's flag; a red background with three thick, wavy lines of blue and white symbolizing the Missouri and Mississippi rivers and at the intersection of the three lines, a yellow circle with the fleur-de-lis in the center.

Mayor Robertson gestured to the guest chairs. Debbie sat down in the spot to the right, the PR flack immediately sitting down in the one to the left. Like a French king, the mayor took his place on the black leather throne placed behind an imposing two-toned wooden desk, espresso-brown panels offset by red-toned trim.

"Well, Ms. Bradley, welcome back to St. Louis," Mayor Robertson began. "How does it feel to be home?"

Debbie smiled and played along with the boosterism. "Really good. It's nice to spend time with my mom."

Mayor Robertson nodded. "Yes, Beth Hughes. She's certainly well known in the legal community. How's her cancer, if you don't mind me asking?"

It seemed, at this point, that people in town knew far too much about Debbie's life. "So far, the news is encouraging. She's had wonderful medical care."

Mayor Robertson nodded solemnly. "We are blessed to have some of the finest medical institutions in the country located right here in our city."

"Indeed," Debbie agreed. Knowing that time was limited, and the press rep would happily usher her out regardless of whether Debbie had asked all of her questions, she did her best to speed past the pleasantries. "So, Mayor Robertson, I know you're an extremely busy man. I really appreciate the fact that you agreed to meet with me."

He smiled, showing off his somewhat lightened teeth. They weren't movie star white; after all, that wouldn't fit in a Midwestern city with union roots. But they'd been lightened just enough to give him a youthful glow.

"I thought that it would be good for us to get acquainted. Perhaps a sit-down with me could help you get off to the right foot in this town. A number of my supporters read your magazine. If I talk to you, I bet they will, too. I'm always happy to help open doors for a fellow St. Louisan."

Quid pro quo, that's what he's getting at, Debbie thought. He would do her a favor, and she would do him a favor. Even though Debbie needed an access pass into the upper echelons of St. Louis society, she'd never stoop so low as to sell her integrity to get it.

"Well, as I said, I really appreciate your time. And there are so many things to talk about. One of the topics on the minds of people who live in our city is the fact that St. Louis continues to rank as one of the five most dangerous places in the country. Don't you think that's hurting our ability to attract new industry, new talent?"

"Fake news," Mayor Robertson said.

"Pardon?" Debbie replied.

"The stat is fake," he repeated with a smile. "Those rankings look only at the boundaries of the city itself, not the metropolitan area. It's unfair to use a population of three hundred thousand to represent an area of two point eight million people."

"That's a valid point," Debbie conceded. "Be that as it may, there are still an awful lot of murders within the city limits every year. There were over two hundred last year. And if our current pace holds, we'll break a record this year. Already, the summer has been deadly. And that doesn't even include other types of crimes. I know from firsthand experience that stolen cars have become an issue of late."

"No one can say for certain how this summer will end up, especially given that we've deployed more officers to the areas where we've seen an uptick in violence. In those districts, we're having officers patrol and walk the streets. We're arranging more community meetings. You see, we need to strengthen our community ties. Unfortunately, trust has eroded. And without trust, we can't seem to get the tips and information we need to protect the people who are being hurt. I want to help them. But they have to help me."

Debbie scribbled in her reporter's notebook. Even though she was taping the interview—as was the PR flack—she liked to have a handwritten backup. Plus, it was easier to check her quote accuracy when she knew approximately where in the interview a statement was made.

Debbie decided to go direct with her questions. "Do you think that crime could be reduced if we could curb the use of so-called community guns?"

The mayor paused. The public information officer chimed in. "Ms. Bradley, can we go off the record?"

Debbie sighed, put down her pen, and turned off her recorder. "Go ahead. I'm listening."

The PR rep spoke. "I'm not sure where you heard that term. But it doesn't apply to St. Louis."

Mayor Robertson spoke. "Where'd you hear about community guns? Flannery?"

Debbie shook her head. "Flannery? Heavens no. I wouldn't describe him as someone who enjoys talking to media, let alone giving us tips."

"I would be very disappointed if I found out that he was spreading disinformation to reporters."

"Do you suspect he's been sharing false information?" Debbie asked.

"I just think that it's only fair I warn you to be careful around Detective Flannery," Robertson said.

"What do you mean?" Debbie asked.

"Flannery has, um, shall we say, a complicated past?"

Debbie pursed her lips to stop herself from asking if that complication included the mayor's wife. "What do you mean?" was all she could come up with.

"For most of his career, Flannery's had a cloud of suspicion over his head. If you need proof, look at the fact that he's still only a detective. I don't know if you're aware of this, but we went through the police academy together. I fully expected him to be the police chief one day."

"What happened?" Debbie asked.

"There was a scandal—though it mostly was kept quiet. Internal affairs never had anything ironclad. Plus, the police union closed ranks around Flannery. His family has deep roots in the department and a lot of pull with the union. If it had been anyone else, he would have been fired."

"Flannery has always seemed like a by-the-books kinda cop," Debbie said.

"Sure. But he really hates bad guys. So much so that some believe he broke the law, you know, reasoning that the end justifies the means. You see, Ms. Bradley, there were some drug dealers who claimed Flannery framed them."

"That happens all the time," Debbie said. "You know as well as I do that if you ask ten people convicted of a crime whether they did it, five will say they're framed. Another three will say the police got the wrong guy."

"In Flannery's case, drugs were found in his car."

"His patrol car? Again, It could've simply been dropped by a suspect."

"No, I mean his personal vehicle," Robertson said.

"Well, he was the one who could've been framed."

"That's what he claimed. Indeed, Flannery was drug tested. No traces of illegal substances. A search of his bank records didn't find any odd deposits. No one could track down any unusually large cash purchases. So if he wasn't using or selling, why were there drugs in his car? The most likely explanation is that he was setting up people to make sure they got convicted. Otherwise, the drugs didn't make sense."

Robertson continued, "Anyway, as I mentioned, he survived the investigation. However, his career stalled. The officers respect him, but the police board doesn't want to deal with the controversy that could come with promotions. But neither do they want to deal with outrage among the ranks if he's let go. See, he exists in a law enforcement limbo, mostly gets shoved into some corner of the department and forgotten. At least until a reporter makes him look like some kinda hero."

The flack stood up. "I'm afraid that's all the time we have for today. The mayor has another meeting scheduled in five minutes."

"But I didn't get a chance to ask much at all," Debbie protested.

"I'm sorry we have to end this now, Miss Bradley. But I did enjoy meeting you. If you have any other questions about our programs and initiatives to keep our great city of St. Louis safe, my office can fill you in on the details."

"I'm going for a run," Debbie announced as she headed toward the front door of her home. "I need to clear my head."

Beth, who'd been sitting on the living room couch scrawling notes in a yellow legal pad, briefly glanced up from her work and nodded. "Don't worry about taking a key. I'll be here."

Debbie bounded down the front steps then put her headphones in her ears. She opened her favorite running playlist, queuing a mix of random songs that helped her set a steady pace.

Lafayette Park was directly across from her parents' home. Established in 1838 and supposedly the oldest park west of the Mississippi River, it was ringed with a black iron fence, each spindle topped with a fleur-de-lis. Debbie had been coming here since she was a child. There were photos of her in pigtails standing on an ornate arched bridge that survived the 1896 tornado, pictures of her father pushing her on the swings at the playground—both of them beaming—a few photos of her leaning against a concrete frog created by sculptor Bob Cassilly, and even a senior prom picture on the old bandstand that she'd reluctantly allowed her parents to take.

Debbie figured she needed at least five laps around the park to shed her funk. Traveling once around the perimeter was three-fourths of a mile. The first go-around she dedicated to letting go of ruminating over her phone call with Sam, a conversation that kept playing in her head.

"My story about the mayor is a dud," Debbie had said when she called Sam from city hall's parking lot after her meeting. "He just wanted to see if I'd play ball. If I'm good to him, he'll be good to me. I floated the topic of community guns. He claimed there was no such thing. But judging by how fast he and his minion reacted, my guess is that there's more to it."

"Of course there's more to it. Good gawd, if biscuit-making, gun-wound-patching grannies in the hood are telling you there's a problem, there's a problem. Either the mayor is very stupid—which is a possibility— or he wants to keep the information quiet," Sam said. "Maybe he's worried that talking about illegal gun violence will land him in the middle of the gun controversy in general. Whatever the case may be, it's worth digging more into the issue."

"But that's still a project that will take some time," Debbie said. "Maybe there's the Flannery angle. It sounds like the mayor wants me to go after his police academy classmate. I mean, he basically accused Flannery of being a dirty cop. But he did it in that way politicians and mobsters like to do, that way of saying something that gives them room to deny that it was the intent of their conversation."

"A dirty cop story would be a big one, if you can prove it," Sam replied.

"I don't have the sources inside to get that one," Debbie answered.

"What about Officer Parker? It seems like she's warming up to you. Why don't you work on her?"

"Maybe," Debbie said, not convinced that the young cop would help her. "But still, I'm not convinced there's a story there. The mayor has a personal motivation for going after Flannery. Maybe Denise Robertson is having second thoughts about ditching her first husband now that he looks more heroic."

"Possibly," Sam said. "But what if the mayor *is* trying to help you with his hints?"

"Are you serious? I haven't spent much time around here but he strikes me as someone who gives to get. He'll lend one half-hearted hand and demand two helping hands in return."

"I won't disagree," Sam said. "But a half-hearted hand is still something. Be that as it may, our owner is happy that you've met the mayor. I took the liberty of telling him. It helps you—and me."

"Ugh, I haven't met this tech benefactor. And you're making me more stressed," Debbie said.

"Isn't that an editor's job?"

The mention of *River City*'s owner, and the fact that he was keeping tabs on her, meant that Debbie couldn't find the anxiety relief she was looking for, even after she finished her first mile.

Plus, she was still annoyed with Mayor Robertson and his public relations officer. And Ada's comment about Chase Laclede had left her unsettled and reminded her of the unresolved issues she had with Christian. Her former fiancé hadn't texted. He hadn't called. Yet he did seem to have time to post comments about news developments on Twitter. At least that's what Debbie had noticed while obsessively checking his feed.

It wasn't until the third mile that Debbie's shoulders finally felt looser, her breathing having fallen into the familiar rhythmic pattern that matched her stride. Instead of fixating on her problems, she started to notice the parents pushing jogging strollers, brisk walkers with hand weights, and the dog walkers.

And then it stopped. Everyone seemed to flee from Debbie's path. A scream was loud enough to be heard over her music. She yanked the earbuds from her ears.

"Look out!" A man on the sidewalk across the street who was walking his dog pointed behind Debbie. She turned to see a car had jumped the curb and was driving partially on the sidewalk. Straight at her. And it didn't show any signs of slowing.

Debbie darted through an opening in the gate and ran behind an old elm tree, hoping it would block the car.

The driver swerved back onto the roadway. The driver's face was hard to see because a baseball cap had been pulled down over his forehead. The front windows were rolled down. But Debbie thought she caught a glimpse of a gun being pointed at her by the driver.

"Fucking bitch!" It was a man's voice. And the car was gone.

A crowd materialized. "I'm fine," Debbie said, her voice wavering as she tried to open the hand that she'd used to clench her phone as she tried to get out of the car's way.

"Did anyone see the driver?" Debbie asked.

"No, but I got a look at his license plate," someone volunteered.

"She was most certainly targeted," Beth said to Flannery. "You can't deny it."

Flannery and Officer Parker appeared at Debbie's house after word spread about the chaos in Lafayette Park. Even though no one had been hurt, residents in the normally quiet upscale city neighborhood were upset that the tranquility had been shattered.

Beth was seated in one of the overstuffed chairs in the living room. Flannery and Parker were on the couch. Debbie stood in the doorway between the living room and the front hall.

"Mom, please," Debbie said, irritated that her mother had taken over the conversation and was dominating the discussion.

"Ms. Hughes," Flannery began.

"Beth," Debbie's mom insisted.

Flannery nodded. "Beth. I'm not going to deny it. However, I think it was probably meant as a warning. Debbie said she thought the driver had a gun. If he truly wanted to get rid of her, he wouldn't have been so dramatic. After all, you have to admit that driving down the sidewalk in a crowded park is far from subtle. No, if he really meant business, he would've just shot at her from his car."

Officer Parker flinched at Flannery's blunt assessment. But Beth's gaze remained steady and focused on the detective as she studied him carefully, searching for telltale signs of betrayal that his words didn't match his thoughts.

"Ma'am," Parker added, "I think Detective Flannery is absolutely right here. She wasn't shot at. And it was a rather big production."

Tired of being talked about, rather than talked to, Debbie chimed in, "Well, if someone thinks that I am easily scared, they don't know me." She looked directly at her mother as she spoke.

Beth pursed her lips, having learned from years of experience that arguing with Debbie would only cause her daughter to dig in even more stubbornly.

Flannery cleared his throat, attempting to cut through the mother-daughter tension. "You both might be interested to know that the car was stolen," he said.

"Gee, there's a surprise," Beth responded. "Are there any cars on the streets right now that aren't stolen?"

It was Flannery who flinched, unaccustomed to sharp rebukes. "I can assure you that the mayor and the police chief are aware of the problem. Ms. Bradley has helped bring that issue to everyone's attention. In fact, I just learned that we'll be rolling out bait cars to see if we can disrupt whatever seems to be going on right now."

"Interesting," Debbie said. "I'm surprised the mayor didn't mention it in our interview."

Flannery shrugged then stood up to leave. "I don't profess to know what is going on in city hall. I'm just a detective."

Parker, taking her cue from Flannery, joined him in preparing to depart. "I can assure you both that we're searching for the car. Although with so many looking, my guess is that it will have been tucked away in a garage. Or we'll find it abandoned on the street."

"Will you at least keep me posted? Let me know if you find anything?" Debbie asked as she opened the front door for their guests.

Parker answered. "Of course."

"What's that for?" Debbie said, referring to a baseball bat in the back seat of her editor's car.

"I thought we could stop by the batting cage on the way home; take a few swings, hit a few balls," Sam responded.

"Seriously?" Debbie asked.

"Of course not," Sam said. "I brought it just in case we have any trouble."

"I'm not so sure that a baseball bat will do much good," Debbie answered.

"Well, I don't own a gun. And even if I did, I'd never bring it to an interview. I've found that folks don't usually like to talk with a pistol around. Doesn't do much for building trust."

She'd called Sam after she'd nearly been run over in the park. Knowing that he had access to the LexisNexis motor vehicle registration database, Debbie gave him the license plate number and asked, "Can you track down the owner?"

"More than likely, yes," Sam said.

But their conversation was cut short because Flannery and Parker had paid the surprise visit to Debbie's home. "I'll swing by in an hour," Sam said after Debbie relayed the turn of events. "That'll give me time to do some research and we can go to the owner's home together."

And in an hour, Sam was at Debbie's house, just as he'd promised. By then, Flannery and Parker were long gone.

"How'd it go with your officer friends?" Sam asked.

"Fine, I guess," Debbie said. "To be honest, I didn't get to ask too many questions. My mom was busy cross-examining Flannery. Though I have to admit it was kinda fun to see him wilt in the face of her onslaught."

Sam chuckled. "I wish I could've been there for that."

"Oh, it was something," Debbie replied. "So, what'd you find out about the owner of the car that tried to mow me down?"

"It's registered to a woman. According to her driver's license information, she's in her mid-forties. Lives in Affton," Sam explained, referring to a solid working-class inner suburb.

"Well, the driver was a man," Debbie said. "So we can rule out the owner, unless she was part of a plot."

"We're about there," Sam said as he turned his car into a tidy neighborhood of homes built in the 1950s and parked on the street in front of a small red-brick bungalow.

"Why don't you let me do the talking?" Sam suggested as they walked up the sidewalk bounded by a freshly mowed lawn. Yellow day lilies bordered the sidewalk, and a statue of St. Francis presided over the front steps.

Sam knocked. Debbie found herself drawing in a big breath then holding it while she waited for a response.

A woman with straight reddish-brown hair that framed a round face and offset her green eyes appeared from behind a curtain that covered a window inlaid into the front door. Her brow furrowed as she looked at the strangers.

"Yes?" she asked loudly so that her visitors could hear her without having to open the door.

Sam's shoulders relaxed. An easy smile spread across his face. His usually gruff voice and sarcastic tone were gone.

"Hello, ma'am. We're from *River City* magazine. I'm Sam Hitchens, the editor. And this is one of our writers, Debbie Bradley."

"I don't want to buy no subscription," the woman said.

"No, we're actually here about a story. We're doing a piece on stolen cars in St. Louis. Now, Ms. Bradley here was almost run over by a car. Turns out that car belonged to you. I'm guessing it was stolen," Sam said, using his most sympathetic voice.

The woman opened the door. She was wearing a faded yellow cotton sundress with large white flowers. "My Lord, I heard! Like I told the cops who was just here, my car's been missing for about a month now. And between us—I didn't tell the cops this—I want it to stay gone. I've already made me a claim on my insurance and used the money to buy an Altima. Now, I don't know if I'm supposed ta let the insurance company know that my car is being driven by some crazy ass fool who's tryin' ta mow people down. My Lord. Do you think he's ISIS?"

Without hesitating, Sam replied, "Hmmm. ISIS. Well, stranger things have happened. But I don't know how much they're much interested in the Midwest."

The woman leaned in and whispered, "We got the Arch. I watch the news. They're coming for us."

"Is that what you told the police?" Sam asked.

The woman nodded. "Yeah. But they weren't interested. They just wanted to talk about the car. But c'mon, they've got the records. I reported it stolen when it happened."

"When was that?" Sam asked politely.

"Like I said, about a month ago. I went to the Savvis Center for a concert," she said.

"Ah, you mean the Scottrade Center? Oh wait, Enterprise Center," Sam said as he tried to remember all the various names attached to the arena since it had been built in 1994.

The woman nodded. "Whatever they're calling the old Kiel now. I can't keep up."

Sam laughed. "I'm with ya. What concert did you see?"

The woman looked at Sam and then Debbie. "Well, see, I went with my old high school girlfriends. We decided to see that concert that had some bands from back in the day. You know, New Kids on the Block, Paula Abdul, and Boyz II Men."

"That was a great one," Sam said. "When they played 'You Got It.'"

"Right! I know," the woman said enthusiastically.

"So, your car was stolen during the concert?" Sam asked.

The woman nodded, leaning closer to Sam. "Boy, were my friends pissed. 'Course, we'd also had a bit to drink. So, at first, I thought I had just forgotten where I parked. We paid twenty bucks at one of those lots that open downtown during concerts and baseball games. Kinda down by the MetroLink tracks."

Sam nodded. The woman continued.

"But then we finally tracked down our space. One of my friends had been smart enough to note it down in her phone. Anyway, there was glass on ground. No Honda. No Betsy."

"Who's Betsy?" Sam asked.

"My Glock. I kept her under the front seat. Locked and loaded, so to speak. Not literally locked in a car safe or something like that, just the safety lock," the woman answered. "If I had it in a safe, how could I get it when I need it? A single woman can't be too careful. Especially when you go downtown. I took my protection. Now I gotta add terrorists to my list of threats: robbers, rapists, and ISIS. I just bought me a new piece last week."

"I understand the fear," Sam said. "After having your gun and car stolen, are you keeping the firearm at home?"

The woman laughed. "Bertha is for the house. Betsy Two is for the car."

"I see. You have two guns. So, have the police found the original Betsy?" Sam asked.

"Nope. And they haven't found my car. But they say it might turn up now."

"Look, I appreciate your time," Sam said as he handed her his card. "If the police call with any news, can you let me know?"

The woman smiled. "I'll think about it. Maybe you'll have to buy me a beer. For being someone with the media, you seem to be all right."

It wasn't until they got back in the car and had pulled out of the neighborhood that Debbie finally spoke. "Oh my God!"

"What?" Sam asked.

"Who are you?" Debbie asked. "Did you go to that concert?"

"Nope. But who do you think had to edit the concert review?"

"You know, I think she sort of likes you," Debbie teased.

Sam smiled. "What can I say? I'm a charming man when I want to be."

Debbie groaned.

"You do what ya gotta do," Sam said before squaring his shoulders back, regaining his authority as an editor. "We'll see what happens. But right now, I'm curious about her gun Betsy. Do you think her stolen gun is the one that is tied to the other crimes you've been tracking? It's been a month. Plenty of time to circulate in the community and wreak a lot of havoc."

"That same thought occurred to me," Debbie admitted. "I guess we'll know when—if—we find the gun. Well, I mean if the police find the gun. And if we find the driver, maybe we find the person who is connected to these shootings."

"Maybe," Sam replied.

Debbie's phone vibrated with a text message. "Huh," was all she said for a moment.

"What?"

"It's from Parker. She says that I should contact the mayor's office to lean on the police department to see if I can do ride-alongs for the bait car sting the SLMPD is planning."

"What are you waiting for?" Sam asked.

15 BAIT CAR

It had taken Debbie longer than usual to get dressed. This was, after all, the first time she'd been invited to a ride-along with the police. And she hadn't had much time to prepare. She'd only just started trading texts with the SLMPD's press contact the day before, when she learned that the bait car experiment was already planned for the following day.

As she stood in front of her closet, Debbie pondered the weather. The outside temperature had been hovering above ninety degrees Fahrenheit for days. The air was thick with moisture, making it even difficult to breathe. She'd always blamed the oppressive humidity on the fact that St. Louis was a city stuck between two mighty rivers, the Mississippi and the Missouri. And when pollution was mixed in with the moist air, physical exertion in the afternoon was a challenge for even the most healthy.

Debbie didn't plan on doing any running during the stakeout, but then again, it was probably wise to plan for every contingency.

The reporter made her way down to the kitchen. "What do you think?" she asked her mom.

Beth, wearing a navy pencil skirt, a cream-colored blouse, and a matching jacket, looked nothing like a recovering surgery patient. Which was exactly the message the lawyer wanted to communicate.

"What do I think about what?" Beth asked.

"My clothes. Do you think I'm dressed to hang out with the cops?"

Beth looked at her daughter from head to toe. Blue jeans, a short-sleeved polo, and Converse sneakers, hair pulled back in a tight ponytail. "You look presentable."

"Really?"

Beth shrugged. "Well, you do resemble a college kid who gives campus tours."

"Thanks," Debbie replied.

"If you were wearing khakis, I might say camp counselor." Beth waved her hand as Debbie grimaced. "Oh, come on. I'm just joking. You're overthinking this. Really, you look fine."

Beth took a sip of coffee before saying what was really on her mind: "Do I need to worry about you today?"

"Are you kidding? The police made it very clear that I'm going to be a distant observer. I don't get to be in the center of the action. The city's lawyers keep mentioning liability."

"Thank goodness for the lawyers," Beth said. "Folks with some sense. And with the series of unfortunate encounters you've had lately, I'd say that they're probably also worried about their officers becoming collateral damage. I don't know that it is too safe for them to be around you."

Debbie sighed. "Perhaps. By the way, how are you feeling?"

"Really good," Beth said with a smile. "I'm trying to ignore the fact that I'll get the verdict about chemotherapy this week. The oncologist said the medical review committee would be looking at my file and making a recommendation. I really don't want to have to go through chemo."

"I know. I don't want you to have to go through it either," Debbie said.

Debbie parked her rental car in the St. Louis Metropolitan Police Department's North Patrol lot. She spotted Officer Parker near the front entrance with Flannery.

Flannery nodded as Debbie approached. "How'd you manage to get an invitation to this shindig today?"

"I think the mayor leaned on the police chief," Debbie lied.

Flannery shook his head. "When it comes to women, the mayor is easily charmed."

Officer Parker coughed. Debbie ignored the jab.

"Well, how will this work?" Debbie asked.

"We have a specially outfitted SUV," Flannery explained. "It's an older model. We'll park it in an area where we've seen a spike in car thefts. We'll leave a purse on the passenger seat. The keys will be inside."

"Isn't that entrapment?" Debbie asked.

"No." Flannery shook his head vigorously. "We are just providing the opportunity for criminals. We're not encouraging them to do something that they wouldn't have already done."

Debbie opened her notebook and scribbled a few lines. "I see," she said.

Flannery continued. "The car doors lock once the bad guys get inside and only we can let them out. They'll be able to start the car, but they won't get too far. We've got a kill switch that allows us to turn off the motor. We'll surround the car and then nab our joyriding thieves."

"Okay. This should be interesting," Debbie said, trying to contain her excitement. "Will I be riding with you?"

"Nope," Flannery said. "You're not going get very close to the action. Not as long as I'm here. You are going to spend some time with Officer Parker." Flannery paused. "And Officer Parker is going to remember that she's with a reporter, right?"

Parker gave a curt nod. "Yes, sir."

Flannery continued. "You and Parker are going to observe from a distance. You can listen to the action on the radio. And once we have everyone apprehended, then she'll bring you over."

"I really hoped I could get a bit closer," Debbie said with her best smile.

"And I really hoped you wouldn't be here at all. And Parker would like to be in on the action. Consider us all disappointed," Flannery said.

"Is it just me, or is Flannery even more of a jerk today?" Debbie asked Parker as they drove to a location near— but not too close—to the bait car.

Parker shrugged. "I don't know what you mean."

"C'mon. You can tell me," Debbie said sweetly.

Parker looked at Debbie's tape recorder and notebook, then pursed her lips.

Debbie said, "Look, off the record. I'm not going to print it. Why the heck is he in such a foul mood?"

Parker found a spot in a park near the bait car, rolled down the windows to try to keep her vehicle from suffocating them, and turned off the engine. All that was left was the sound of passing cars, some kids playing in the park, and the squawk of the police radio as cops talked about getting into position for the sting.

"Off the record?" Parker asked again.

"Absolutely," Debbie said.

"He isn't happy that you're here."

"That much is obvious," Debbie answered.

"Rumor is that he and the police chief and the mayor got into it over this plan. So much so that people outside of the chief's closed office door could hear them arguing. Gossip says that Flannery called the mayor's idea a publicity stunt. He said that he couldn't guarantee your safety. Seems he's concerned that the shooting at your car the other day wasn't random, especially after the incident in the park."

Debbie rolled her eyes. "I can take care of myself."

"Of course," Parker said. "Paternalism is alive and well, especially in law enforcement. Anyway, you know there's bad blood between the mayor and Flannery anyway," Parker added. "You know, that whole ex-wife thing. And to think they were once close friends."

"They were buddies?" Debbie asked.

"A long time ago," Parker said.

"Before Mayor Robertson stole Flannery's wife, I presume?"

Parker nodded. "Obviously."

"Was it also before Flannery was accused of being a dirty cop?" Debbie asked.

Parker cleared her throat. "We don't talk about that," she said as she turned up the police radio. "Let's go back on the record. You might be interested in the conversation that is taking place over the police radio."

Debbie flipped open her notebook and began scrawling down the clipped conversation that drifted through the radio. More than once, Flannery came on to remind the cops that a reporter was listening to the entire conversation. Most of the banter was benign, Debbie thought, juvenile insults punctuated with a reference to someone's mother hurled among officers to relieve the boredom. When the insults became too salty, Flannery was once again on the radio. Occasionally, the chatter would stop when pedestrians would near the car. It was almost as if Debbie could feel them holding their breath. But then those walking would continue on.

After a while, even Debbie found it dull. Her primary distraction was a group of kids throwing rocks in the park. She guessed they were around twelve or thirteen. Just the sort of kids Teen Alliance would want visiting their center rather than wasting time out on the street. A few of them spotted Parker and Debbie sitting in the car. One of the kids in the group started to head over to their car when a friend grabbed him by the arm and shook his head.

"What's that all about?" Debbie asked.

"You know that whole 'idle hands and devil's workshop' saying, right? At least one of them was trying to figure out if we were easy targets," Parker said.

"Easy targets for what?"

"Probably to rob us. Steal our car. Play the knockout game. Who knows," Parker said.

"The knockout game?" Debbie asked.

"Roaming gangs of kids looking to prove their street cred. The object of the game is to knock an innocent person down. They'll punch and kick the poor sap who happens to be in the wrong place at the wrong time. One old guy walking home from the market was killed that way."

"But they're so young," Debbie said.

"Don't let their youth fool you," Parker said. "Anyway, one of them has figured out we're undercover cops."

The noise of the radio interrupted Parker's warning.

"Looks like we might have a winner," a voice called out. "Two suspects, male, probably late teens or early twenties, skinny white guy with short hair wearing a wife-beater and an African-American guy, bigger, in jeans and a gray T-shirt. They walked past the vehicle. Turned around and gave it a second look."

Flannery's voice chimed in. "Are they approaching?"

"Yeah, Detective. One is opening the passenger door. I think he saw the purse."

"I see it on the camera," Flannery said. "He's got the bag in his hand. Seems to be rummaging around in it."

"I see that as well," said one of the officers. "His buddy seems to be keeping an eye out. Oh, looks like the dude with the purse just found the keys."

"Everyone sit tight," Flannery said. "If they turn on the ignition and move it away from the space, I'm going to hit the kill switch. When I say go, I need you to arrest them nice and neat. Remember, they could be armed."

Debbie held her breath. She couldn't see what was happening. All she could do was listen to the crackly voices over the radio.

"Go, go, go," Flannery shouted. "Kill switch activated."

The sirens sounded. Debbie could hear them wailing through the radio as well outside, as if in stereo surround sound. But she couldn't see anything.

"What's happening?" Debbie asked. "Can't we go over now?"

"My orders are clear. You're not to be allowed on the scene until Flannery says so. And I'm not about to cross him," Parker said.

"Well, at least tell me what it is you think they're doing," Debbie pleaded.

"They'll circle the car and get out with their guns drawn. Three cop cars, I think."

Debbie could hear the screech of brakes through the radio. "Hands up! Hands up!" Debbie heard through the radio.

"I'm unlocking the doors now," Flannery told his officers.

"Get down on the ground!" Debbie heard through the radio. Then it was silent. The silence seemed to last for ages, but it was only a few minutes.

"You can bring Ms. Bradley over now," Flannery said.

Parker threw the car into drive and stomped on the gas.

"It must be killing you to babysit me," Debbie said. "I'm sorry about that. And I appreciate your tip."

"I'll have other chances to be in on the fun," Parker said as she swung the car down a few blocks and brought it to a quick stop.

They were closer to the action than Debbie thought.

Two teens were bent over the hood of a car. Their hands were being cuffed behind their back. Flannery was barking orders to make sure the scene was secured. One officer was told to keep an eye on the people who had gathered on the sidewalk to gawk.

"Keep her back!" Flannery shouted to Parker. "I don't want her contaminating any evidence."

Debbie gritted her teeth. She'd been good. She'd followed directions.

Pop. Pop. Pop.

"Get down!" Flannery yelled.

Parker ducked behind a car. Debbie stood still, frozen in place. She could hear the bullets but couldn't tell where they were coming from.

Ting. Ting. The bullets were ricocheting off the car next to her. She could see the suspects had been pulled to the ground. Several officers had taken cover behind the car doors that had been left open.

Flannery came bounding toward her. "Get down!" he yelled.

He leaped into the air and tackled Debbie, who landed with a thud on the hard asphalt.

The shooting stopped.

Parker appeared from behind the car, looked at Debbie, and then looked at Flannery before yelling,

"Officer down! Officer down!"

16 OFFICER DOWN

When the shooting stopped, the detective rolled his weight off of Debbie. His face was pale. His eyes darted about, still searching for the threat.

Debbie sat up, dusted herself off, and spotted the blood on her clothes. "Oh my God!"

"If you'd just listened," Flannery said, a barely perceptible pant punctuating the end of his sentence. "Gotten down when I told you to." His face grimaced as he sat up. He reached down to press one of his pant legs that was shifting from tan to crimson as Debbie watched.

"I'm sorry. I'm sorry," Debbie said, unable to look away from the liquid spot that was expanding in size. "I froze." She looked up at the circle of officers who had gathered around them. "We need an ambulance! Where's an ambulance?"

Flannery snorted. "There's already one on the way. I heard Parker calling for it. Thank God someone keeps her wits about her under fire."

The cry of sirens could be heard in the distance. Whether the sound was from an ambulance or police officers who'd heard the "officer down!" call over the police radio and were now rushing to the location, Debbie wasn't sure. But as the cacophony grew louder, it seemed likely that there was more than one car on the way.

"You saved my life," Debbie stammered.

"You shouldn't have been here," Flannery said, his voice with the breathlessness of a runner in mid-jog, only he wasn't moving. "I had a bad feeling about this from the very moment I was told of this publicity stunt. You're bad news, Bradley."

The crowd of blue parted to let a paramedic inside the circle.

"No artery. Just meat," Flannery said as the first responder was already at work cutting the cloth away from the wound.

The paramedic exposed the detective's thigh. "Yep," he said tersely, "a deep graze."

Debbie watched as the paramedic administered first aid while another rolled over a stretcher.

Flannery noticed that Debbie was suddenly pale.

"She's gonna go down," he barked as he pointed to the reporter.

An officer steadied Debbie.

"Just take a few breaths," Flannery told Debbie, his voice only slightly softer than before. "Look, this wound is nothing but a fuckin' annoyance. I probably won't even miss any work. And that stinks. I could use a paid vacation. Hell, I'd take an unpaid vacation so long as I could get away from you for a while."

Flannery was helped to his feet by the paramedics. When they tried to lead him to the gurney, he balked. "I'm not laying down on that thing, I can climb into the back of the ambulance. I'll sit."

With a paramedic at each arm, Flannery shouted a few last orders. "The suspects need to go back to the North Division and questioned. Find the shooter. With the officer down call, there should be a swarm of officers here in no time."

"Parker!" Flannery shouted, finding some energy in his reservoir of lingering anger at the mayor. "Take Bradley back to the station. Get her to her car. And for god's sake, make sure she doesn't linger around here. Who knows what she'll write."

Parker hesitated. "I said to get her out of here," Flannery growled.

Parker put her hand on Debbie's shoulder to guide her away from the scene.

"And Bradley," Flannery shouted, "before you go to the office, I think it would be wise if you went home and changed your clothes."

Debbie looked at the dark circles on her jeans and the red spots on her white Converses.

A smile crossed his face. "I imagine your mom is going to give me an earful about this one. At least you get to deal with her wrath first. I'm going to hide from her at the hospital for a while."

At home, she was safe. And, at least for now, she was alone.

Debbie peeled off the clothes she'd picked out only hours earlier and tossed them into the corner of her bathroom. She turned the shower on as hot as it would go, waiting for the steam to start rising from the tub. Her bare feet didn't register the air-conditioned chill of the white tile floor made up of tiny hexagon shapes that had been popular at the turn of the century and then lovingly reproduced during one of her mother's exacting renovations. Instead, her attention was focused on the medicine cabinet mirror above the white enamel basin. She stared blankly at her reflection, not recognizing the hollow-eyed woman who stared back. Eventually, the stranger dissolved in the bathroom fog.

Debbie put her hand into the stream of water, flinching only when she realized just how hot it had become. She adjusted the temperature, waited a few more minutes for her shower to cool down, then stepped in.

As the water fell over her hair and down her face, the shouts of *officer down* bounced off the inside of her skull. As Debbie closed her eyes and rubbed shampoo into her hair, it was Officer Parker's horrified face at seeing Flannery's wound that appeared.

Debbie reached for her bath scrubber, smeared it with more body soap than one person needed, and rubbed her skin until it turned bright pink. When her body could no longer tolerate her efforts to wipe away blood stains that seemed stuck in her head, Debbie hung the scrubber back on a hook and positioned her body squarely under the cascade of water, surrounded by steam that rose up from tub.

The heat was suffocating. So much so that Debbie found herself falling forward, catching herself by placing her hands on the far wall of the bathtub. It was there that she hunched over like a suspect across the hood of a car. It was only when the water turned to ice that Debbie found her balance.

You've got work to do, she told herself. *Pull yourself together and get on with it.*

She grabbed her robe and dried her hair with one of the extra towels. Her gaze rested on the heap of clothes in the corner. *I'll deal with that later.*

Debbie opened the bathroom door and stepped into the cool hallway. She threw on a pair of old sweatpants and a T-shirt. Her hair was a wet tangled mess that she didn't bother to comb. Instead, she made her way down the stairs and to the kitchen, where her laptop waited on a cabinet.

Just get your thoughts down. Edit later. Just get your thoughts down.

When her fingers touched the keyboard, they began to move haltingly. Within a few minutes, they effortlessly picked up speed. All that she'd experienced that day was somehow spilled onto the screen while Debbie watched, detached and fascinated. She had no idea how long she sat there. All she knew was that she wasn't pushing words out, they just appeared.

When she'd finished the description of Flannery climbing into the ambulance, sitting down, and stoically refusing to flinch as an IV was inserted into his arm just before the ambulance doors were shut, Debbie's hands stopped. That was enough for today. She already knew it would be another blog post. A firsthand account that would later become part of the story she'd weave for the print magazine.

Debbie grabbed a mug to make tea and caught her reflection in the microwave door. Her hair had dried into a tangled mess, as if she'd been sleeping on the streets for weeks.

Her phone vibrated on the table. She'd been semi-conscious of the fact that it seemed to be shaking nonstop ever since she sat down in front of her computer. But only now was she ready to face her callers.

The most persistent contacts were from her editor and her mother. Phone calls and texts that seemed to get more insistent and irritated when Debbie didn't reply. She knew she'd held them off long enough. She'd save the hardest call for last.

Debbie dialed Sam first.

"Where have you been? I've been trying to reach you for hours. I even called the police department to see if you were okay."

"I'm done," Debbie said.

"What?"

"I'm done. I wrote a post about today. It's ready to go. I just need you to edit it. If you think it's good enough, can you post it? If it isn't ready, I'll work on it tomorrow. Oh, and I've got photos. You pick the ones you like. I've uploaded them into our shared folder so you can choose."

"Forget about the piece for a moment. How are you?"

Debbie inhaled then exhaled loudly. "I don't know. The only thing I know is that I needed some time alone. I didn't want to talk to anyone. I just wanted to process my thoughts. I needed to write. I didn't want to contaminate what was in my head, the sights, the sounds, the story in my head. I needed to write it all down before I started talking."

Debbie paused. "I just needed to be left alone."

Sam was quiet. "I'll take a look. Maybe you should take a few days off. The print magazine with your story about Jarrett will be available tomorrow. Would be a good time for you to take a short break."

"Maybe," Debbie said as she heard a set of keys landing in the bowl just inside the front door. Her mother's footsteps sounded angry. "Look, I gotta go," Debbie said just as her mom appeared in the doorway.

Beth's eyes were blazing with anger as she strode up to her daughter.

Debbie put down her phone on the cabinet, her arms going limp along her body as her shoulders sagged. Beth stepped forward and wrapped her arms around Debbie, saying nothing. It was only then that tears tumbled from the reporter's eyes.

17 THE DAY AFTER

"Tough break for Detective Flannery," the mechanic said to Debbie when she arrived to pick up her car. Beth had given her daughter a ride to the garage. The repairs had been finished, and Debbie could finally reclaim her wheels.

It was the day after Flannery had been shot. It had been the top story on all the local TV news stations. Reporters from every channel had been stationed outside the hospital, hoping to get a glimpse of the detective, but had to settle for statements from the police chief who paid a visit.

"I think he saved my life," Debbie said.

The mechanic stapled together the service summary as well as the invoice. Then he tugged a medal out from under his shirt, rubbed it, and then slipped it back under his collar. "We all need a guardian angel. But I feel sorry for yours."

Debbie mustered a half smile.

"I hope the next time I see you, it's for an oil change," he said as he handed Debbie the keys to the Civic and pointed her to the lot.

After driving a newer model rental car, she noticed all of the things that her Civic lacked. And it looked tired, a little beat up. A little defeated. As Debbie adjusted the driver's seat to fit her frame instead of the mechanic's, her cell phone rang. She checked the number. Her stomach tightened, and it felt as if someone had wrapped a hand tightly around her heart and squeezed it with as much might as could be mustered.

"Hello, Christian," was her shaky opening.

"Hey, ace," he replied. "I wasn't sure you'd answer."

"Why?"

"Well, one, because it's me. Two, because it looks like you're a one-woman news machine in St. Louis. Your story about the bait car and the shootout. That's some fine work."

"Just lucky. Right place, right time. Or wrong place, wrong time, depending on how you look at it," Debbie said.

"Same ol' Deb," Christian replied. "When are you going to just admit that you're a good reporter? You can dig up facts and can wordsmith it into a riveting piece. Your article is making the rounds in the newsroom here. Everyone is surprised what you've been able to produce in such a sleepy mid-sized town."

"Thanks, I think," Debbie replied, miffed at the gratuitous jab at St. Louis. Sure, it wasn't D.C., New York, or L.A., but it was her hometown.

"How's your mom?" Christian asked.

"Surprisingly good," Debbie answered. "She hasn't taken much of any time off work. She's so stubborn."

"Like mother, like daughter," Christian said. "*Cabezona.*"

Debbie laughed. "I haven't been called pigheaded in a while."

"So," Christian said before clearing his throat, "you coming back?"

Debbie shut her eyes.

"Look, I'm running late for a meeting," Debbie said. And she was. Chase had left her a message the night before, after he'd read the online version of her bait car story. He'd asked her to stop by his office the next day.

"No problem, I just wanted to compliment your work," Christian said before he hung up the phone.

Debbie gripped the steering wheel and put her car into drive. She had work to do.

The greeting was awkward.

Chase extended his hand to Debbie, but a handshake seemed too formal. After all, they had gone to dinner together and were past the meet-and-greet stage of a relationship. But a hug didn't feel right either; too familiar for the reporter and lawyer who were still not completely sure whether the other could be trusted.

"You've been busy," Chase said after Debbie took his hand. He gestured toward a conference room. "Stakeouts, shootings, and a steady stream of stories."

Debbie shrugged. "I swear to you that my life is mostly a collection of boring bits. Things will quiet down soon, you'll see."

"I'm not so sure," Chase answered. "You kinda remind me of someone who keeps accidentally stomping on nests of red wasps hidden in ground ivy. You should be careful. You've been able to outrun your threats so far. But you may be outnumbered soon."

"How can I stop when I don't even know what I'm doing?" Debbie replied. "I just ping from crime to random crime. The only thread that seems to tie it all together is St. Louis."

"Sometimes we try to create connections in things that aren't connected," Chase cautioned. "How often do people try to come up with a story that explains happy or tragic events by stringing together random actions and concluding there was a larger theme that ends with a statement that 'it was meant to be'? Maybe you're trying too hard to piece together something that isn't a puzzle. Maybe each act of violence is just arbitrary and capricious."

"I've considered that, too," Debbie admitted. "Perhaps I'm trying to manufacture a logical explanation for an illogical world."

"That would be understandable. And maybe there is something more going on. I don't know. But I do know one thing."

"What's that?"

"You're an outsider," Chase observed. "In the dangerous neighborhoods you're exploring, it is going to be awfully hard for anyone to want to stick their neck out for you."

"Don't you think I know that?" Debbie said.

Chase shrugged. "You seem rather hardheaded to me."

"Funny, that's the second time today I've been called stubborn," Debbie said, recalling her brief conversation with Christian. Damn him, she thought. Christian was the last person she wanted to think about right now.

"You said in your message last night that you had some information for me," Debbie said, switching the subject.

"Yes," Chase said. "I guess you could more accurately call it a proposition."

"I'm listening," Debbie said.

"My young client Joshua Lucas is a good kid," Chase said.

"A so-called good kid who killed another good kid driving a stolen car," Debbie reminded him.

"And what about all of those privileged kids who do stupid things and get away with it? Drinking and driving. Buying and using illegal drugs, then getting behind the wheel, killing someone. Affluenza. It doesn't make any of it right, but if your family doesn't have money or power, the law will do everything it can to crush you."

Debbie frowned. "You don't think I know what you're talking about? I've seen how privilege can act as a get-out-of-jail-free card. Or, at the very least, get a lighter sentence. But all I can do is tell stories about them. I can't fix them."

"I disagree," Chase replied. "I called you last night after I read the Flannery blog post. But then I got my copy of *River City* magazine this morning. I read the piece you wrote on Jarrett. I think your story will make a difference for that young man. I think you also have the power to make a difference for Joshua."

"How so?"

"What if I were to let you interview Joshua's grandfather?"

"I can't guarantee that the story would be sympathetic. I can only write what I learn," Debbie said.

"It isn't my job to convict or acquit. Plus, it's complicated because I'm a witness."

"I know that. But you're already following the story. You're part of the story. Joshua's grandfather wasn't at the scene of the accident. He doesn't have any information that is directly relevant to the alleged crime. But he can tell you a bit about Joshua."

"Even if Joshua's grandfather sits down with me, I can't guarantee that it would turn into a story."

"I understand," Chase said. "But it could be string that you'd be able to use in your final story on the outcome of this case."

"Okay, let me know where I can find him," Debbie said.

Jarrett rushed down the front steps of his grandmother's house before Debbie's car had come to a stop at the curb.

After putting her Civic into park, Debbie rolled down the passenger window. "It looks like somebody is excited to see the story."

Ada, who had just stepped out onto the porch, called back. "He's been pacing in front of the living room window ever since you called to ask if you could come over."

"Jarrett, the magazines are here on the front passenger seat. Could you grab them and bring them in?"

Jarrett, who'd been standing next to the car with his hands thrust into his hoodie pockets, tried to feign an indifferent shrug. But there was a smile on his face. "Sure," he said.

"Why don't you come on inside," Ada said to Debbie. "I just finished frying some bacon for BLTs. My neighbor's growing some tasty tomatoes in her backyard. She always gives me her extras."

"You know you're not going to have to work too hard to persuade me to eat," Debbie said as she headed up the walk. "I'm just glad that I was able to find you both here."

Ada held the door open for her grandson and the reporter.

"Well, you see, there's been some going-ons since we last talked," Ada explained. "And I see you've been getting into trouble, too."

Debbie shook her head. "I'm fine. Now, Detective Flannery isn't so good."

"My nephew says he'll recover," Ada volunteered.

Switching the subject, Debbie asked, "What are these going-ons you mentioned?"

"Oh, nothing necessarily bad," Ada said as she led the way back to the kitchen, where Jarrett was already sitting with one of the magazines open. "The lady at Teen Alliance, um, Mrs. Owens, and the mom of Chase Laclede met with my daughter and son-in-law. Seems Mrs. Laclede wanted to pay for Jarrett to go to some sort of class to study for that college test."

Jarrett interjected, "The ACT."

Ada nodded. "The ACT. Now, Jarrett's a smart boy so I don't know why he needs to take an expensive class."

"I understand," Debbie said. "It does seem counterintuitive, but those classes can give Jarrett some tips and tricks for how to improve his score a bit. And every little bit can mean more money is knocked off tuition. I also took classes."

Ada gestured for Debbie to sit down in a chair at the kitchen table. Then she placed a sandwich in front of her guest, along with a glass of sweet tea. "Doesn't seem very fair to the kids who can't afford those classes."

Debbie nodded. "I know. It isn't."

Ada wiped her hands on a kitchen towel then reached for a magazine. "Anyway, since Jarrett's taking these classes, he needs a ride out to the county. And his daddy decided it was time for him to start doing some more driving. So Jarrett comes over here and borrows my car. He complained it is a granny car, but you know what they say about beggars."

Debbie laughed.

"Anyway, he can drive to his classes. And part of the deal is that he then usually picks me up some groceries at the store on his way home."

"That's a nice trade," Debbie said.

"Yeah, I guess. But I worry about him driving by himself. But his parents are thinking more and more of Jarrett being off to college. They're trying to give him more independence so that living on his own doesn't come as such a shock."

Debbie looked at the young man who was engrossed in the story. He seemed too young to be driving on the crazy highways of St. Louis. "I've never really thought about how hard it must be to give kids a set of keys." Taking a bite of her sandwich, Debbie added, "Now, I know you can't wait to read the story. I'll eat. You read."

The kitchen fell into a comfortable silence. Ada and Jarrett each had their head bent over their own copy of the story. Debbie sipped her tea and savored the taste of beefy heirloom tomatoes, crispy bacon, cold iceberg lettuce, and mayo on white bread. She looked out the kitchen window and into the tidy backyard, circled with a four-foot chain-link fence. She could see the raised garden bed of Ada's neighbor, popping with all sorts of fresh goodness. *I wish people could see this part of my city*, Debbie thought to herself, *rather than always being bombarded with the scary headlines that say St. Louis is the most dangerous city in the nation.*

It was only when she was aware that two sets of eyes were looking at her that Debbie pulled her daydreaming gaze away from the backyard.

Jarrett wore a bashful smile. Ada dabbed at the corner of her eyes with the same kitchen towel she'd used earlier.

"I don't know that we deserve all that fine writing," Ada said. "I really don't know what to say."

Debbie waved her hand to bat away praise. It was something she didn't handle well. "I had the easy part. I just write what I see."

"You see things, Miss Debbie, that a lot of people don't," Jarrett said.

"I wouldn't be so sure about that, Jarrett. I feel like I'm in the middle of something but I can't quite make it out."

Ada shook her head. "Maybe you just need to be patient. It'll come."

"Perhaps," Debbie said. "I'm not really known for my patience. But while I'm here, I wanted to get your thoughts. I'm going to see the grandfather of Joshua Lucas in just a bit. Chase Laclede set it up. What do you think I should ask him?"

"That poor man," Ada said. "I knew his wife. She did a lot for this community. They deserved a grandson like Jarrett. But they got Joshua."

Ada fell silent. "I don't know what you should ask him. As the preacher said at the funeral, we got babies killing babies. Just be gentle with the grandfather. He's an old man. And he tried. But when you get older, when you have kids, you realize how little control you have over separate human beings," she said as she reached out and touched Jarrett's hand, "even if they're your kids, or grandkids."

18 BROKEN

The bungalow had seen better days. The pale yellow trim was peeling away from the wooden windowsills. Mesh screens that had once kept mosquitoes out of the home were torn, flapping when the occasional breeze found its way through the narrow spaces between the tightly packed brick houses. A rusty air conditioner hung out of a side window, coughing and rattling.

Debbie knocked on the front door. After a few moments, she heard shuffling on the other side.

The door opened wide rather than just a crack. An old man, his shoulders stooped and his head bent, peered at Debbie. He seemed too defeated to be cautious.

"Ronald Lucas? I'm sorry to bother you," Debbie began as she introduced herself. "I think Chase Laclede called you. My name is Debbie Bradley. I'm the writer who'd like to talk to you about your grandson."

"I just sat down to have some dinner. You can come on in. Call me Ron, please," the old man said as he opened the screen door to let her in.

The front room was tidy. A gold sofa with brown sunflowers faced a large television. Vanna White rotated blocks with letters on the screen. A microwave dinner, still in its black plastic container, the clear film peeled back, sat on an orange metal tray. A fork on top of a hand towel was next to the makeshift meal.

In the background, a windup clock ticked loudly, the noise competing with the sputtering air conditioner. The old man picked up a remote, fumbled for a few moments with the buttons, first turning up the volume before finally decreasing the sound.

"I'm still tryin' to get used to this darn TV," Ron said as he eased himself down on the couch. "I liked my old one. But when they switched something, it no longer worked. Something about analog and digital. My old TV worked just fine."

Debbie sat down on a chair covered with the clear fitted plastic that had been popular in the sixties. "Please, please go ahead and eat. I don't want your food to get cold."

The man waved his hand dismissively. "This stuff tastes nothing like my wife's cooking. I'd probably stop eating altogether if it wasn't for Joshua. I force food—if you can call this food—into my body to stay strong for him. Otherwise, there's just not much left for me here on this earth."

Debbie couldn't help feel guilty about the BLT she'd just finished at Ada's. "TV dinners don't beat a home-cooked meal. That's for sure."

Ronald Lucas pushed the tray aside. "So Mr. Laclede told you about me."

"Actually, I saw you over in juvenile detention a few weeks ago, talking to your grandson," Debbie admitted. "And I've heard about you and Joshua's grandmother from a variety of people. Seems you and your wife are held in high regard."

"I have no idea how we got Mr. Laclede. I know he's worth more than I could pay him. I had a little bit of money saved from my wife's life insurance that I had taken out a long time ago. I'd been saving it for my grandson. A college nest egg; a tiny one, but a start." His voice trailed off before getting strong again. "That Mr. Laclede. I wish Joshua would learn something from him."

"From what I've heard, you're a pretty good role model, too. I understand you're a veteran. Vietnam," Debbie said as she pointed to a Purple Heart mounted in a glass case on the wall.

He waved his hand dismissively. "What ya gonna do? You get drafted. You gotta go. Then you just try to stay alive. I got hit by some shrapnel after a buddy stepped on a land mine. He didn't make it. I did. Random luck, both good and bad, that decided I'd be standing where I was that day, and where he was that day."

Ron fell quiet for moment, his eyes resting on the Purple Heart. "My wounds brought me back home. I didn't have any college, but I was a veteran. Once all the shrapnel was taken out of my body—arms, legs, neck—and healed up, I got a job with the St. Louis Public Schools as a janitor. That's when I met my sweet Sarah. She was a kindergarten teacher. And thank God that little ones are always making messes that require a janitor."

The old man smiled and rubbed his eyes. "I fell in love with her as soon as I saw her. She was the kindest woman I'd ever met. To this day, God didn't make anyone more gentle. But boy howdy, you bet she could keep those little ones in line without ever even raising her voice. The kids just loved her. They wanted to please her. Her classroom was sunny and bright. Just like she was. After being in a war that was none of my damn business, it felt good to be around all that hope."

Ron stood up. He winced. "You can take bits of metal out of a man, but the body ain't never gonna be the same again." He walked over to a cabinet and took down a photo. "This is me and Sarah on our wedding day."

"She's lovely. And you look so handsome," Debbie said as she gazed at the old man as he once was, so long ago, standing next to an attractive woman with a bright smile.

"Sarah always said she loved my strength. She felt safe with me. And I worshiped her. Heck, I wasn't the only one. Her students did too. You know they named a garden after her?"

Debbie nodded. "I heard."

"She'd be so disappointed in me now. I thought I could protect her from heartache, but I couldn't. You see, our daughter, Joshua's momma, caused my wife a world of hurt."

"What happened?" Debbie asked.

"We had a good little life. We bought this house. We had a baby girl. We was real happy. But then crack cocaine swept through our world. When my daughter was teenager, she got caught up on it. We tried so hard to get her cleaned up. I finally had to kick her out. My wife was heartbroken. Our daughter ended up on the street doing God knows what for drugs."

Ron was silent again. He pointed to another photo. "That's Joshua's momma before the bad times."

He sighed. "But then, she somehow made it into her early thirties. She was locked up for a while, that probably helped. She met a guy, Joshua's dad. Our daughter got pregnant, but the couple started doing drugs again soon after Joshua was born. My wife took the baby. And when Joshua came to live with us, my Sarah found new meaning, new joy. Joshua was her chance to make things right. It was good to have a young'un in the house. I think it was her chance for a do-over, you know? A chance to fix the mistakes she felt she made with our daughter. 'Course, she wouldn't listen to me when I told her that our daughter's getting messed up in drugs wasn't my wife's fault. But you know how mothers are. They think everything is their fault."

"What happened to Joshua's mom?" Debbie asked, not sure she wanted to know the answer.

"Well, when Joshua was five, his momma was found dead. Murdered. I always thought it was Joshua's dad. But the cops didn't have nothin'. My daughter's murder is still listed as unsolved," Ron said.

Debbie could sense that he didn't want to share the details of his daughter's death. She'd look them up later. Perhaps Flannery knew the full story.

"Anyway, when my daughter died, my wife's heart just couldn't take it. She had a stroke. And then another. She was gone before Joshua turned six."

Ron wiped at a tear from his eye with a cloth handkerchief he'd pulled from his pants pocket. "I made a vow to my wife that I'd take good care of the boy. I thank God every day that he spared her from experiencing this latest mess. The boy is locked up. And even though he says he found the car, nothin's gonna change the fact that an innocent girl is dead."

He sighed. "I'm tired. I don't know how long I can keep going. Any strength I got left has to be coming from my wife beyond the grave. I let the love of my life down. I shoulda kept a better eye on him."

Debbie looked into the man's eyes. "It isn't like you can keep a child under surveillance twenty-four hours a day. Especially a headstrong teenager."

Love, Debbie thought, *between a man and a woman, between a parent and a child, between a grandparent and a grandchild, could be uplifting or devastating—or both.*

The sky was growing dim. It was time to go home. Debbie was drained. "I'm sorry that you're having to handle all of this alone. I imagine that your grandson is relying on your strength—the very quality that your wife admired so much."

Ron shook his head. "What do ya think will happen to my grandson, Miss Bradley?"

Debbie shook her head. "Honestly, I don't know. I think the one thing that is in your favor is that he's a juvenile. If the judge doesn't certify him as an adult, he's may get a second chance. But I can't imagine that he's going to get off with a slap on the wrist. As you said, someone was killed."

"That's what Mr. Laclede keeps saying," Ron replied.

Debbie stood up. "I should be going now. Thank you for your time, Mr. Lucas."

The old man walked her to the door. "I got nothin' but time."

As Debbie walked down the steps, she wondered if she could bring something by later. Maybe some fresh tomatoes. Maybe some of Ada's cornbread. Ron Lucas was broken. Good food wouldn't fix that. *But doesn't he deserve some small pleasure to give him a break from his world of pain?*

She looked back at the front door, but it had already been closed. Debbie imagined Joshua's grandfather throwing his cold, untouched TV dinner in the trash.

Debbie unlocked her car door, climbed inside, strapped on her seatbelt, then put her key in the ignition.

That's when she felt a firm push to the base of her skull.

"Keep both hands on the wheel and drive," a voice commanded.

Debbie looked in the rearview mirror. All that she could see was a dark mask and the outline of a gun pointing at her head.

"Stop," the person in the backseat commanded. To add emphasis to the order, the barrel of a gun was pushed against the back of Debbie's head.

The journalist had been directed to drive to an abandoned industrial area just north of downtown. Her headlights and the faint glow of distant office buildings were all the illumination Debbie had to guide her car. A river barge blared in the distance.

"Put it in park," her carjacker barked.

Debbie did as she was told, all the while racking her brain for an explanation as to how someone managed to get into the backseat of her car. She'd locked her doors. There was no sign of her car being broken into while she'd been inside interviewing Joshua's grandfather.

Stop it, she told herself. Figuring out how someone managed to get in was the least of her worries. The more pressing problem: How was she going to get out of this alive?

Her phone was in her purse. But her bag had been snatched almost immediately by the stranger with a gun. It was now in the backseat.

"Look, I'll leave my keys in the car. You can have my purse, my wallet, my credit cards. I'll even give you the PIN numbers. Just let me go," she pleaded.

The barrel of the gun swept left to right against her skull. "Get out."

Debbie opened the door. Gravel crunched under her feet. She tried to turn to look at the person who'd kidnapped her. Judging by the huskiness of his voice, she assumed he was taller and wider than she. The shoulders broader.

"Nope, turn back around," he ordered. "Put your hands above your head. Spread your legs."

She felt hands grabbing her around her waist. Debbie gasped. The hands slid down her torso and then along the inside of her legs.

"Stay where you are," the carjacker commanded after the pat-down. "And don't turn around."

Debbie did as she was told. With her hands still in the air, a mask was thrust in front of her. "Put this on."

She hesitated. Would it be better to run and risk getting shot at? Or should she put the mask on and wait for another opportunity to escape?

The kidnapper pushed her sharply in the back, her body falling hard against her car. "Don't make me shoot you here. Because I will. Now, put the hood on."

The hood was a burlap bag that smelled of coffee beans. There were no holes for her eyes, or for her nostrils. Once she had pulled it over her head, her hands were grabbed and pulled tightly together in front of her body. She felt a zip tie go around her wrists and then it was cinched with just a little bit of wiggle room between, though not enough to turn her hands and pull them from the constraints. Then she was led by her forearm back to the car and shoved into the backseat.

She was now the passenger instead of the driver.

"Lie down," the kidnapper ordered before slamming the door.

Debbie felt the car start and heard the gear shift move.

"How did you get into my car?" Debbie asked, her voice muffled by the burlap.

"Easy. I had a key made."

"But how?" Debbie said, coughing as she tried to ask the question, the sack choking her when she tried to talk.

"You haven't always had your car with you since you've arrived in St. Louis, now have you?"

Debbie's stomach knotted. *Flannery.* Why had she followed his suggestion for a mechanic so blindly?

"You've really been a thorn in my side. In everyone's side."

"Are you working for Flannery?" Debbie asked.

The man snorted. "Always asking questions you shouldn't be asking. Your curiosity gets you into trouble, doesn't it?"

"How did you find me?"

"We've got our ways of tracking you. Or at least tracking your car."

"You put a tracker on my car?" Debbie said before convulsing into a stream of coughs.

The man didn't reply.

She had to get away. Her purse had to be somewhere in the back seat with her. Could she find it and get her phone? Or her tape recorder at least? It wouldn't be easy. Her hands were behind her back, and she could see nothing. She was lying face down across the back seat, having been shoved in face first. Her head was turned to the side. And she managed to tuck her legs under her belly. Perhaps if she could just use one leg to feel around on the floor.

As she gently poked around, she felt the bag. It was closed. There was no way she'd be able to start her tape recorder with her feet, even if she could get inside her purse to activate it.

But at least she knew where it was.

"You had to go sticking your nose into business where it didn't belong," the driver said. "If you'd just let things be, you'd be at home right now with your mother. Funny, isn't it?"

"What?" came Debbie's muffled reply.

"You probably thought that when you returned to St. Louis, there was a chance you'd wind up attending your mom's funeral. But now, it looks like she's going to have to go to yours—that's if they find your body."

The image of her mother, grief-stricken and alone, flashed in her mind. And how would Christian react? Would he be filled with sadness and regret—always wondering what their lives could have been together? Debbie wondered. Or, after a respectable period of mourning, would he close the chapter to their relationship and move on?

The car stopped. Debbie heard the engine switch off. The driver opened the door.

It was hot and muggy outside, and the bag made breathing even more labored. Each breath left the area around her face moist. She felt lightheaded. *Slow. Breathe. One. Two. Three. Four.*

Debbie heard the passenger's door open and felt someone yank at the waistband of her jeans. Her body slid across the back seat, and she felt herself falling to the ground.

"Jesus! Why did you have to bring her here?" a woman said. The muffled voice sounded familiar, but

Debbie was having trouble placing it. And the lack of oxygen was making her lightheaded.

"Shut up!" It was the driver. "You kept screwing things up. I finally took matters into my own hands."

"So what are we gonna do?"

The driver responded. "You're gonna get one of the guys to leave her car out on the street, one of those places in the city where carjackers love to leave their rides. Then someone from the crew is going to tip off the neighborhood kids that there's an abandoned car with keys inside. They're gonna take it for a spin. Just like that young punk did with that Audi."

The woman, who was standing several feet away from Debbie, asked, "And does she have a gun in there? Like the Audi did? Wouldn't it be beautiful if her bullets were the ones doing all the killing?"

Audi? Debbie thought. *The woman with the Civic who was worried about Isis had Betsy. But Hank Frederich said nothing about a gun. Or did he lie?*

"I doubt it. She's too much of a libtard for that. I did a body search. Turned up nothin'," the carjacker said.

The woman responded, "Well, we still need to go through her purse, pull out her wallet, tape recorder, notebook. I don't want them lying around. And you'll need to get rid of the phone—but make sure you leave it as far from this place as possible. In fact, you should've already gotten rid of it. Who knows what kinda tracker she's got on it."

Debbie felt a hand grab her by the upper arm. She was being yanked up off the ground and pushed forward. "Hmmm. She was pretty," said the man. "Seems a shame to waste something like that. Why don't you let me have a go at her before you finish her off?"

His hands rubbed her shoulders and moved down her back, cupping her ass. Debbie jerked away.

"Cut it out, you Neanderthal," she heard the woman say. "The last thing we need is for your DNA to be discovered on her body. I can guarantee you that the medical examiner will do an especially thorough job because if her body is found, the press is going to go crazy. Not just local press, national press. And the medical examiner hasn't been bought—yet. We're still working on that."

Hands touched her breasts. Debbie jerked again. "Pity. Seems like such a waste."

"I said cut it out. You men are all pigs. Disgusting," said the woman impatiently. "C'mon, we got work to do."

Debbie was pushed forward. The gravel gave way to what felt like concrete. A door slammed, and the noise echoed. She had to be in a large space.

"Who's that?"

There was now a third person added to the mix. Debbie recognized it as well. A male voice. But because she couldn't see, her own loud breathing and the muffling properties of the sack all combined to make it difficult for her to get a clear read on the voices.

"That reporter—that snoopy one," the carjacker said.

"Jesus Christ," the newcomer answered. "I didn't sign up for this. It wasn't part of our deal. What are we going to do with her?"

"She's got to be handled," the carjacker said.

At least adrenaline blocks the pain, Debbie thought. *But for how long?*

She'd been dragged out of her own car, dropped to the ground, then shoved into a room and pushed down onto what she believed was a concrete floor without warning. With a bag over her head, she felt the assaults after they happened, rather than anticipating the impacts.

Now she found herself alone, fantasizing about punching the guy who dared touch her without permission. *Fuck that piece of shit. I'm gonna bring him to his knees with a crowbar to the crotch, then maybe a second whack just to make my point. And a third whack just because I'll enjoy it. Then I'm going to take his picture. Then I'm going to write about him.*

To fulfill her revenge fantasy, Debbie knew she had to escape.

She was lying on the floor where she'd been shoved before a door had slammed, leaving her alone. She'd landed on her right shoulder, at least saving her head from a knockout blow.

No doubt she already had bruises and cuts. If something was broken, she didn't know it yet. So it couldn't be too broken. *I need to see.*

Debbie bent her knees to her forehead, leaned forward, and grasped the bag covering her head between her legs.

Debbie slowly pulled her head back. The first try moved the bag a few inches. She opened her knees and grasped the bag higher up now that more of it was free at the top. It took four of the movements before her face was finally free.

Debbie gasped. The bag was off. She could finally take a deep breath. As she filled her lungs with oxygen, her eyes began to adjust to a room with two sources of light. One was the sliver of moonlight seen through a broken window. The other was from the golden glow of a crack at the bottom of the door that Debbie presumed had been slammed only moments earlier.

She looked around the space. It was likely once a factory clerk's office. Only now, there was nothing in the space except an empty metal shelf and pieces of glass from a shattered fluorescent light. Aside from distant voices and the sound of her breathing, she only heard the occasional drips of water into a puddle.

She had to get out. But first, she had to get up. Without the use of her hands, it wasn't going to be easy.

She scooted so that her back was against a wall to use as leverage. Bending her legs and pressing upward and back, she slowly slid up the wall into a standing position.

Debbie crept awkwardly to the door and pressed her ear against the metal. She couldn't hear anything. She tried the knob. It turned, but the door wouldn't budge. It had been bolted shut from the other side.

The window. She crossed the room to inspect the broken panes. She'd have to somehow make it up to get through the window and past the shards of glass that were clinging to the frames. *This will have to be my last resort for escape.*

A rat scurried over Debbie's feet. She stifled a cry of shock.

What am I going to do? Think, think, think.

That's when the door rattled.

Debbie shuffled to the farthest, darkest corner possible.

The movement of the bolt was barely audible. A smooth slide rather than a hard click. The door opened slowly and not too far, about ten inches judging from the light that filled the gap; just enough to let a thin person through. Debbie could see the shadow of a person entering the room, but the back light meant she couldn't make out the face.

The shadow stopped, as if it was scanning the room trying to find her. It moved away from the door and toward the center of the space.

"Miss Debbie?" the voice whispered.

"Jarrett!?" Debbie replied.

19 BETRAYED

"Oh my God, Jarrett!" Debbie exclaimed, trying to keep her surprise muted to a whisper.

"Shhh," Jarrett said.

"Jarrett, please. Please don't tell me you're mixed up in all this?" Debbie hissed.

"No! Are you crazy?" Jarrett replied. "I'm straight up here to save you."

"Save me? Jesus. You're the one who's insane. You should get outta here. Save yourself. Or get help. This is no place for a kid," Debbie said.

"I'm not a kid. And I'm not leaving without ya," Jarrett said. "If you hadn't noticed, you're in some serious sh..."

"But how?" Debbie interrupted. "How did you find me? And how did you get here?"

"Easy as a day in school," Jarrett said. "Those bike GPS trackers that some guy donated to Teen Alliance. No one really paid attention to them because kids in my area don't ride bikes. Too easy to be a target for a mugging. Miss Darlinda didn't mind if I helped myself to more than one. I ended up taking several. I've been tinkering with them. And then you kept running into trouble, so I dropped a tracker under your front passenger seat the other day. When you had me grab the extra copies of my article."

"But still, how'd you get here?"

"My phone is synced with the tracker. That's how the bike tracker works. I don't have the fanciest phone, but thanks to my parents always worrying about my whereabouts, it still gets the job done. And I admit I kinda like spying. Even though the signal is pretty weak, I can sometimes catch you near me. You're out a lot—and you're in a lot of places that you probably shouldn't be. Anyway, when I was coming home from the ACT prep class, I spotted your blip near me. So, since I've got the car now, I decided to check the accuracy of my setup. That's when I saw you come out of some old man's house. I passed right by you. Thought I'd stop and say hi. But that's when I saw the dude in your backseat."

Jarrett continued, "I followed you. But I had to stay way back. A black kid driving in the bad part of town doesn't raise red flags. But when I saw you turn down this old road, I knew I couldn't keep going. They'd see me. So then I just had to park and trust my phone. The signal isn't exact, but it's close enough. I got here about the time they were done arguing about what to do with you."

Debbie blushed in the dark. Jarrett probably saw the guy feeling her up. *Why am I embarrassed? I didn't do anything wrong.*

"Why in the world didn't you call the police?" Debbie asked.

"That's my backup plan. I hoped that I could find you real quick and free you and you'd be so grateful that you wouldn't tell on me. If I call, my uncle will find out that I was following you instead of going straight home. Then my parents will find out. Do you know how much trouble I'll get into? The wrath of God in the Old Testament ain't nothing compared to what my Granny and my mom might do. There'd be no more going out. No more car. It would be full-on ugly."

"We've got bigger problems than worrying about you being grounded. Can you call now?"

Jarrett looked at his phone and then examined the room. "Coverage in here sucks. Concrete and metal in the middle of nowhere. There's not much reception 'til we get outside."

"Well, let's figure a way out of this place so you can call. But I'm not going to be much use without my hands," Debbie said. "You got something to break this zip tie?"

"Nothing on me. But I think I know how to get you free," Jarrett said.

"How do you know? You've tried it?" Debbie asked.

"Naw, but I watched a YouTube video," Jarrett said. "My math class gets dull. And the teacher doesn't bother me because she knows I'm already ahead."

"I'm not sure whether to be happy about hearing all of the stuff you've been up to, or to be thankful," Debbie replied.

"Here, give me your wrists," Jarrett said. He moved the band's locking mechanism so it was lined up with her thumbs. Then he pulled the band as tight as it would go, making Debbie wince. "Now, you're going to have to lift your hands up over your head then quickly drop your elbows to your side. It may take a couple of times, but it is supposed to snap."

"Seriously? Supposed to?" Debbie asked.

"I've never done it. C'mon. Give it a try."

Debbie raised her hands.

Jarrett whispered, "You gotta use all your might when you pull your wrists down. According to the guy on the video, the lock is the weak part. It should break. As my granny would say, 'You gotta believe.'"

Imagining the revenge she wanted to take on her carjacker, Debbie transferred the force she imagined she'd use to hit him into the sharp downward thrust of her arms.

"Oof," she said when her wrists slammed into her stomach, the tie remaining steadfast.

"One more time," Jarrett said. "I bet you weakened it."

Debbie lifted her arms again. This time, as she brought her arms down, she imagined punching Flannery in the face.

Her hands broke free.

The doorknob made a slight rattle as someone gripped it but hadn't yet turned it. A female voice called out, "Who unlocked this?"

"Quick, try to hide behind the door," Debbie whispered to Jarrett.

"I said," the female voice aimed toward the deep recesses of the factory. "Oh, never mind."

Debbie put her hands behind her back, pretending the zip tie still held her fast.

The woman entered.

"You!" Debbie cried out. "How could you?"

"Now why did you have to go and take your sack off?" Officer Parker asked angrily as she picked the burlap bag up off the floor.

Debbie took two steps back and avoided looking to the spot where Jarrett was hiding. It was dark but the reporter still feared that a clumsy glance could expose her misguided-but-well-meaning rescuer. "Why are you doing this?" Debbie asked.

"Shut up," Parker said, as she moved closer. "And stop moving. You can't get away from me."

"But, please, can't you just answer my question?" Debbie said, moving as far from the door as possible, while trying to figure out what to do next.

"You've already heard the reasons. You're in the way. And we have work to do," Parker said.

"What kind of work?"

"Entrepreneurial and, let's say, street cleaning. I'm a part of a group of smart entrepreneurs and good cops," Parker claimed.

"Good cops don't kidnap journalists," Debbie said.

"You've heard that the end justifies the means, right?" Parker replied.

"The nuns who taught me in school were adamant that wasn't true. Sister Eleanor claimed doing something bad to achieve something good was unequivocally wrong. How we achieve our goals is just as important, maybe even more so, than the final outcome."

"You're naive. And so was Sister Eleanor," Parker responded. "I bet she'd be singing a different tune today. The end is the only thing that matters, no matter how you get to it. If it takes some lying, stealing, some cutting corners, some looking the other way, supporting useful evildoers, who cares? All that matters is the end result."

"I happen to believe that if the means are corrupt, no end can sanitize it," Debbie said.

"No wonder everyone hates the media. Besides, I don't care about stealing cars."

"What are you talking about?" Debbie said.

Parker sighed. "You're getting on my nerves. The story starts with cars. When people don't pick up their towed cars from Ace's lot, for whatever reason—maybe they have no money to pay impound fees, not enough cash to cover the deductible to get a car running; some people just downright disappear—anyway, when those things happen, the tow lot sells the cars, with the city's blessing, so long as the city gets a cut. But the tow company figured out that some cars fetch more cash. And if they could just make cars vanish without ever being recorded as towed to the lot, then there'd be no slice for the city. Even more money for Ace Towing. They've already got the distribution network. Why wait for the product when you can make cars just vanish? Stolen but never recovered."

"Was the Audi part of this?"

Parker put her hands on her hip. "You can't make every car disappear. That would start lookin' too fishy. So sometimes a mechanic in our network will make a duplicate key and add a tracker to the vehicle. Those cars disappear. We might bring 'em here or to another one of our secret sites. The owners report the stolen cars but, because they've disappeared, they never get recorded as having been towed. We scrub the VIN and sell it to a black market syndicate that can move the cars, even out of the country."

Parker stepped closer.

"But the Audi's parts were also worth something. Plus, luxury cars are harder to make disappear. So, our mechanic made a duplicate key. We picked up the car and left it in an area that has a reputation on the streets for stolos—stolen cars. Punks get in, leave their fingerprints all over it, crash it up. They take the blame and do time in juvie, we get the car."

"So Joshua Lucas was just in the wrong place and the wrong time making the wrong choice?"

"You could put it that way. Those kids are terrible drivers, which makes them perfect for our scheme. And they're not the best decision makers. We want the cars to be wrecked enough so they aren't repaired. But if that doesn't happen, well, at least the car goes back to the mechanic, who can inflate the repair prices and skim some insurance money. With a kickback to the towing lot, of course."

"But Rainaa Mercer died! And that mom was shot!" Debbie said.

Parker shrugged. "Unfortunate. Collateral damage. But again, the end justifies the means. This is a war. Sometimes innocent people die. And her death is outweighed by the fact that Travis Hunt also died because of that Audi. And Roberto Simmons is in jail right now. One thug dead, one thug locked up. Plus the dude that was shot during the drug deal outside that abandoned building."

"You lost me. The Audi wasn't involved in those deaths."

"Man, for being such a hotshot reporter, you're slow," Parker said. "Around here, people were getting worried that you were close to finding us out. Turns out you didn't have much of a clue, even though you kept showing up at all the wrong places at precisely the right time."

Parker continued, "The gun. The gun that the Audi owner left in his car. The gun he didn't report missing. That's where I come in. You could call me a gun fairy. We often find guns in these cars. Everyone's carrying nowadays. I remove the guns from the cars and then leave them in a place where bad stuff happens—and there are no cameras. The shit bums always find the weapons. Always."

"So that's why you haven't been ratted out by an informant? No one has seen you? But why would you want to give bad guys stolen guns?" Debbie asked.

"What better way to get rid of an addict than to give them so much product they overdose? Same for the criminals. Flood the area with the guns and they just start shooting one another. Then I don't have to rely on an unjust justice system that lets someone off the hook because of a technicality."

"It's called constitutional rights, not a technicality. It's called beyond a reasonable doubt standard."

"Words," Parker said. "Just words. Even if a bad guy didn't commit the crime, they're still bad. And my method sweeps them off the street."

"And Joshua Lucas?"

"He's on his way to being bad. We're just speeding up the process. The quicker he goes bad, the faster he's removed from law-abiding society."

"But how'd you get mixed up in all this?" Debbie asked while noticing that Jarrett was starting to move from his position. "I mean, you have a good reputation. You're a rising star in the force. And you're supposed to be smart."

"I am smart. That's how I noticed that there seemed to be something fishy at Ace Towing. Fresh cars on the lot. But I hadn't heard much about the thefts in our weekly status reports. I asked Hawkins where they came from. He was his usual lazy, stupid self. He'd mutter that they're stolen cars. Yet, I couldn't help noticing some were like really expensive, Mercedes and stuff. Cars I would've remembered. It just didn't add up."

Jarrett moved a step from the door. Debbie coughed. "Did you say something to Flannery?"

"Yeah. He told me I was just imagining things. And that Hawkins was an idiot, you couldn't rely on what a buffoon like that would say because he doesn't think. But I kept digging. I guess we're a little alike in that regard. Eventually, Hawkins cracked, told me the full story, and offered me a cut. He said they had some heavy hitters backing them and providing cover."

"You accepted?"

"Well, it wasn't about the money, not really. Because so many car owners are packing guns, and they're not taking care of them, well, I could fight some bad guys and make a little extra cash."

"Who are the heavy hitters that are part of this?" Debbie asked.

"Enough questions. Time to get you to your next destination. Your last destination."

There was no more stalling. Debbie lunged toward Parker, who was now less than an arm's-length in front of her. Because Parker didn't suspect Debbie's hands were free, the reporter caught the cop by surprise, managing to trap the officer's arms against her side.

Jarrett jumped from the shadow and locked one arm around Parker's neck, trying to put the cop in a sleeper hold.

Parker let out a cry. Debbie hoped that the cop's co-conspirators thought it was coming from the hostage rather than the captor.

Parker dropped to the ground, then slumped over.

Debbie felt the woman's pulse. It was faint.

"How'd you know how to do that?" Debbie asked.

"My uncle. Remember, he's a cop. He showed me some stuff. He was worried about me getting picked on since I'm a nerd. But I know we don't have much time before she wakes up."

A man entered the room and shut the door behind him. "Holy shit," he said.

Debbie and Jarrett turned to see who they'd have to fight next: Flannery.

Jarrett and Debbie stood up, moving away from Parker's unconscious body. Instinctively, Debbie pushed Jarrett behind her. Flannery pulled out his handcuffs.

"Why are you doing this?" Debbie asked. "I trusted you. At least let the kid go."

"I'm not a kid," Jarrett grumbled as he stepped out from behind Debbie.

"Quiet," Flannery commanded as he bent down to check Parker's pulse, and to remove the officer's gun. Satisfied she was still alive, just out cold, Flannery looked around the room, spotting a rusty radiator along one wall.

"I didn't see this coming. Pity," Flannery said to no one in particular as he grabbed Parker under the armpits. "C'mon. I'm strong. But I was shot recently, you gotta give me a break. We need to handcuff her to that radiator so she can't warn the others. I could use a little help."

Jarrett stepped forward.

"Jarrett, get away from him," Debbie said.

"I'm here to help, not hurt," Flannery snapped. "Take her left side," Flannery said to Jarrett. With the detective on the right, the two pulled Parker toward a radiator that no longer provided heat but instead served as a home to many generations of spiders.

Flannery looped the cuffs around an iron pipe that disappeared through the floor.

"That'll hold her for now. But she's gonna wake up soon," Flannery said. "Anyone got a rag or something?"

"There's a burlap sack that they had over my head," Debbie volunteered.

"That'll do. At least it will muffle her shouts, but we don't have much time," Flannery said as he put the bag over his officer's head.

"I don't understand," Debbie said. "Aren't you involved in all this?"

"I've been working with the feds on the public corruption part of this," Flannery said.

"Public corruption?" Debbie echoed.

"Yeah," Flannery said. "Either of you hurt?"

Jarrett and Debbie shook their heads no. "How'd you find me?" Debbie asked.

"Tracker," Flannery said, his answers clipped, each word costing precious seconds. "That time you went to my mechanic. You were closing in on the people we've been trying to bust. My guy confirmed there was already a tracker on your car, probably done when your car was towed to Ace."

"For fuck's sake," Debbie cursed. "You, Ace Towing, Jarrett. Is there anyone that doesn't have me under surveillance?"

Exasperated, Flannery answered, "Hey, Google, Facebook, and god knows what other apps you have on your phone are tracking you all the time to sell you stuff. At least I'm just trying to keep you safe."

"Um, maybe someone should ask me before tracking me," Debbie said.

"So that's how the kid got here?" Flannery asked.

"Bike tracker," Jarrett said, his voice full of pride.

"Okay, you both found a way in here to rescue me, so let's get the rescuing going. How are we gonna get out?"

"This room is off the factory floor. Mostly, there's stolen cars out there. The rest of the bunch is in another office on the other side of the area."

Parker started to groan.

20 BETRAYED

Flannery looked at Debbie. "You ever use a gun?"

"No. Not a fan of firearms," Debbie answered.

"Well, I'm not giving a gun to a kid. Take Parker's weapon," Flannery said as he demonstrated how it should be used. "Don't use it until you absolutely must. We can't have a case of friendly fire."

Debbie took the weapon, surprising herself at how quickly she was willing to grab it. And how much more powerful she felt with it in her hand. *I need to keep it away from Jarrett, and protect him. The world would be a sadder place if he didn't make it to college. His end can't come in an abandoned factory.* At least that was the rationale she came up with.

The cop cuffed to the radiator started to struggle.

A voice from a distance called out, "Parker! What's taking you so long?"

"Get behind the door with me," Flannery ordered, pushing Debbie and Jarrett flat against the wall. "We've got the element of surprise. Once I get his attention, when he's focused on me, you two need to run. I called for backup before I came but I warned them it was a hostage situation. So they're probably somewhere out there now trying to figure out what's going on, waiting to hear from me. But they aren't going to wait much longer. Get out there but keep your hands up as high as you can. Jarrett, tell them who your uncle is. And for god's sake, Bradley, ID yourself right away. They're not gonna want to shoot a journalist."

The door opened. "Dammit, Parker, where are you?"

A man stepped through. As he turned toward the muffled figure cloaked with a sack, Debbie identified the profile of Quinn Hawkins.

"What do we have here?" he asked as he reached his hand out and brushed the captive's breast.

The figure jerked. "Fuckin' pervert!"

"Parker?" Hawkins said.

Flannery stepped forward and pressed his gun into Hawkins's back, smack dab in the center of his shoulder blades. "I suggest you put your hands in the air. Don't even dream of turning around."

That's when Debbie and Jarrett slipped out the office door.

"You've gotta lead the way," Debbie said. "I don't know how to get out of here."

The area where she'd been held hostage gave way to a cavernous space. Dark tracks were still mounted to the ceiling, a suspended railroad that once moved steel sheets high above the factory floor. But the machines on the floor that once fed the metal were long gone. In their place were rows of cars, some intact, some stripped, some hovering in the space between. It was a chop shop that would draw little attention since the nearest neighbors consisted of rats and barges; a staging area where whole cars and parts of cars could be shipped easily and without notice.

"Holy crap," Debbie whispered. No wonder so many people were complaining about stolos. She followed Jarrett's lead, crouching behind each car, stopping occasionally so Jarrett could check for approaching feet while Debbie kept watch above.

Parker's gun was cold against her lower back. She'd slipped it into her waistband, a spot where she could retrieve it quickly. Debbie didn't trust herself to carry the weapon in her hand, afraid she might accidentally unlock the safety or panic and pull the trigger, shooting the wrong person. Plus, as they made their way across the floor in a crouched position, it took all of her effort to stay balanced and move silently. She didn't need the extra weight of a gun in her grasp. It would just make her clumsier.

"We've got product to move!" Debbie heard a man shout. She knew that voice. But she still couldn't place it.

Jarrett stopped, looked back at Debbie, and pointed to the floor. Debbie looked under the car. She could see a pair of black dress shoes approaching, the dust from the gravel outside only slightly smudging an otherwise flawless polish. She noticed navy, cuffed dress pants that had been tailored to break neatly at the top of the shoe. Whoever it was, he had money. A tailor. And taste.

If they stayed frozen, the man would be able to glimpse the pair hiding behind a car. There was no going back. And staying where they were wasn't an option.

Debbie reached back and pulled out the gun Flannery had given her.

"Go!" she whispered to Jarrett. "I'm right behind you. I got you covered."

"You better follow me," Jarrett said, part plea, part warning, just before he took off for the entrance.

Debbie turned back around to see Flannery peering at her through the door.

"Robertson, come and get me!" Flannery shouted to the mayor, the owner of the dress shoes Debbie had just seen.

"Detective?" Robertson shouted back, approaching the spot where Debbie was frozen.

Jarrett had made it to the entrance. Flannery was stepping out of the office. Robertson focused his attention on his one-time partner. Debbie knew that Flannery was doing this to increase her chances of escape.

Debbie was torn. She could stay and help Flannery. Or she could watch Jarrett's back.

"Go!" was the lone word she heard from Flannery. Her legs obeyed his command.

That's when she heard gunshots.

21 RUIN

"Don't shoot! Don't shoot! Don't shoot!"

Debbie could hear Jarrett screaming the words as the pair emerged from the factory. His form was a dark outline set against the blinding glare that had flooded everything in front of them. His hands were as high in the air as humanly possible.

"Drop your gun!" came a voice from other side of the wall of light.

"Miss Debbie, your gun!" Jarrett shouted.

"Freeze! Drop your gun!" the voice commanded.

Jarrett halted. Debbie followed his lead. "Your gun, Miss Debbie, your gun! You're gonna get us killed!" Jarrett yelled, even as the shots inside the factory continued to ring out.

As if waking from a stupor, Debbie realized she still had Parker's service revolver in her hand, even though it was held high above her head. She tossed it away, the firearm landing with a thud in the gravel.

"Get down on the ground!"

Jarrett dropped down face first, his arms and legs spread out from his body.

Remembering Flannery's advice, Debbie shouted, "I'm a journalist. He's a hostage. A kid. His uncle's a cop."

Debbie could hear Jarrett's muffled voice shout, "Sergeant Davis."

Amplifying his message, Debbie repeated the name: "Sergeant Davis!"

"Jarrett?" Debbie heard a man yell.

"Get down on the ground," another voice commanded.

Debbie fell to the ground, imitating Jarrett. Police officers rushed forward. Some passed Jarrett and Debbie, sprinting toward the factory. Four surrounded Jarrett. Another four fell on Debbie.

The reporter felt her hands being pulled behind her back. For the second time that night, she was bound at the wrists. This time, with handcuffs. Hands patted her down. Then she was lifted to a stand. She was at the center of this drama, and yet she also felt removed from it, her consciousness rising up from her physical form, viewing the scene like a spectator even as her brain continued to jot down notes.

"I'm Debbie Bradley. That's Jarrett Compton. I was kidnapped. Jarrett, Detective Flannery, they tried to help me. The detective is still in there. Officer Parker. Mayor Robertson. Bad guys," Debbie said as quickly as possible, trying to get them to understand what was going on.

She could hear the chopping blades of a helicopter overhead. A spotlight beamed down on them from above. Jarrett was also spitting out the story as fast, and as disjointed, as Debbie.

"Get those handcuffs off my nephew!"

Debbie watched as Jarrett's hands were freed. A man, presumably Jarrett's uncle, pulled the boy close, his words part anger, part fear: "What the hell are you doing here?!"

"That's the reporter, the one who wrote about me," Jarrett said, nodding his head to Debbie.

"Uncuff her," Davis bellowed.

"You gotta help Detective Flannery. He's outnumbered in there," Debbie pleaded.

"Get them back," Sergeant Davis shouted, referring to his nephew and the journalist. "Out of the way."

Debbie and Jarrett were pushed forward and away from the factory, their legs following the commands of the hands that had grabbed their arms. Finally, once behind a line of cop cars, they were freed with a command to get down. The pair could finally stop and catch their breath.

Once again, Debbie tried to explain what was happening inside the factory. Trying to sort the good guys from the bad.

The shooting stopped.

"Person down!" she heard someone shout.

"Come out with your hands in the air. You're surrounded."

A cacophony of shouts swirled about the reporter. She was trying to identify the voices, parsing them into the categories of helpers and hostage takers.

The media should arrive any minute now. They're probably already on the way. And she couldn't help but think: *This is my story.*

Debbie peered over the hood of a squad car, trying to figure out what was going on even as she briefly

236

registered her possessiveness over a story she'd fallen into so deeply that she'd never come out objective on the other side.

Parker and Hawkins emerged from the factory, their hands in the air.

A group of six officers surrounded Parker and Hawkins. At least ten cops ran past them, into the factory with their guns drawn.

"Get a stretcher in here," someone shouted.

Debbie raised herself to a full standing position, watching as Parker and Hawkins were handcuffed.

A medical bed on wheels went inside the abandoned building, along with a couple of paramedics. Where they'd come from, how they got there, Debbie had no clue. Events had overtaken her. Now, all she could do was watch from behind the line of safety.

Three officers emerged from the factory. Behind them, a stretcher. A sheet covered the body. All Debbie could make out were the shoes. They were the dress shoes she'd spotted under the car inside the factory.

"Oh my God," Debbie said to everyone—and no one.

Five more figures appeared. Two uniformed officers flanked each side. The man in the middle: Detective Flannery.

When Flannery emerged from the factory and started barking orders, relief softened Debbie's tense face. He was bleeding, yet again. This time, it seemed that paramedics were rushing to put pressure on his upper arm.

Flannery shouted, "Where's the writer hack and the kid? I sure as hell hope no one shot them!"

"We're here!" Debbie and Jarrett blurted out in unison.

The pain flowed as the adrenaline ebbed. Every part of her body ached. After being pushed, dropped, and pulled like a stuffed Raggedy Ann, it was no wonder that she was bruised and battered. Fortunately, nothing was broken.

Flannery continued barking even as he was being led to an ambulance. "Call Beth Hughes. Get a car to her house. Get her down here," Flannery ordered. "Sergeant Davis!"

"Yo, Detective," Jarrett's uncle said.

Flannery replied, "You've got one very stupid, very smart, very brave nephew."

Debbie saw Jarrett beam.

"Yeah, his grandfather was the smart one. He gets the bravery from me. I'd say the stupid part is my sister, but that don't tell her I said that," Sergeant Davis shot back.

"Ha!" Flannery bantered back. "You know where I'd lay the stupid."

As Flannery was about to step into the ambulance he stopped and laughed. "Bradley?"

"Yeah?"

"If there's such a thing as karma, you're going to get a taste of it. Let me know how you feel after the reporters descend and shove a mic in your face."

Jarrett's parents flanked either side of the boy protectively as he gave a statement to the police. The sergeant stood next to his sister, scowling whenever the cop who quizzed his nephew asked a question too severely.

Debbie watched the scene from afar. She'd been pulled away from the teen so that they could give their accounts separately, neither tainting the other's recollections. But she occasionally paused as she recounted her story so she could see how Jarrett was faring.

She also couldn't miss the line of television news vans had been kept at bay behind yellow tape. Debbie knew they were waiting for her—just as she had waited to ask questions of many other victims. Would she try to slip away in a squad car or stop for an interview? She still hadn't decided.

A police SUV squeezed past the media, stopping near Debbie. Beth Hughes emerged from the back seat. The lawyer, clad in a faded pair of Levi's, a white T-shirt, and running shoes, took long strides toward her daughter. The only thing that betrayed her mother's legendary cool was how rapidly she crossed the distance, her hair getting a lift from the haste that she made.

It was first time Debbie noticed how even authority figures like officers parted as her mother passed. More than one man stole a quick admiring glance at her middle-aged mom before returning to his task.

And suddenly, Debbie felt her mother wrapping her arms around her. Beth's hands were trembling, the only clue Debbie had that her mother was totally and completely freaking out.

"Daniel called me," Beth said.

"Daniel?" Debbie answered.

"Detective Flannery. He called me from the ambulance. Can you believe that? I could hear beeping noises and paramedics, and he's calling me."

"He saved my life," Debbie said. "Well, he did—with the help of Jarrett."

"Daniel said you've done some amazing work. He also said you've been through a lot. You might be a little bit shaken up."

"I don't know how I feel," Debbie admitted. "Right now, I feel numb. It's as if I'm watching me as an actor in a movie."

Beth nodded. "Normal. Very normal reaction to a traumatic event. I brought you something. I don't know if it will help you regain a sense of control, of balance," Beth said as she reached into her purse.

"Oh my God. Thank you!" Debbie said as she reached toward the reporter's notebook and pen that Beth had brought.

Debbie scribbled Kidnap #1 on her notebook's white cardboard cover. She flipped it open and began to write.

22 CONNECTIONS

The seven days following Debbie's ordeal had melted one into another.

After the police had finished questioning Debbie on the night she was kidnapped, she stopped for a brief media interview. She praised Jarrett and Detective Flannery, and she didn't shy away from naming her hostage takers.

Her mother, without being asked, turned from lawyer to PR handler, using her quick thinking to deflect hard questions. Sensing an opportunity, Beth played up her role as a concerned mother to gracefully edge her daughter out of the view of the cameras and into a police SUV waiting to take them home.

Debbie's conscience felt better. She had cooperated with the media. And yet, she'd also been able to hold back some of the juicy details about motive for her own story. The reporter knew it would leak out soon enough. But perhaps if she went home and wrote, she'd be the first to fill in all the details of that night. And she was the only one who could fully tell her own story.

Unable to sleep when she arrived home, Debbie wrote, a first draft being ready for Sam that next morning. She fell asleep for a few hours, got up, and reviewed his edits. Her story about the tow truck scandal, the flood of stolen guns on the street, was out by the end of the day.

Over the next few days, even as she recovered from home, Debbie continued to work the phones—and her sources. When indictments were handed down, the public information officer for the cops made sure she got a copy.

Debbie continued to write from her room. Sam continued to edit and then publish the latest installment on *Crime Beat Girl*.

What Toni Parker had said was true. The corruption started with the tow truck company. And it had started before Toni Parker ever joined the force. The tow truck company had figured out a way to skim money from the city through tows. And the more they made, the greedier they got.

Mayor Robertson had figured it out when he was on the force. He used the information to his own advantage. Like so many politicians, his supposed principles were no match for his lust for power. When he found something he wanted, nothing would get in his way.

He used his cut to make donations to other politicians, to help them get elected. And they, in turn, helped him move up the ranks, from alderman and then to mayor. All the while, he still gave Ace Towing a helping hand.

Off the record, Flannery told Debbie that he had long suspected Ace Towing and Robertson. But the detective was damaged goods, having been framed long ago for shaking down drug dealers. A setup that Flannery suspected was caused by Robertson. A way to stop Flannery's ascent, and to perhaps get the woman Robertson wanted, Flannery's wife.

Like Robertson, Parker had also figured it out. "When a good cop loses faith," Flannery told Debbie by phone, "the results can be disastrous. There's a ring of truth to those comic book superhero/supervillain stories, you know? Only I was too blind to see her slip. I blame myself for that."

Parker had said nothing, invoking her Fifth Amendment rights against self-incrimination.

But Quinn Hawkins had been singing like a hairy fat man in a hot shower.

Parker's description of the car ring had been accurate. And Hawkins said it had been Parker's idea to push the guns that owners left in their cars back out onto the street. It was her signature contribution.

Chaos theory and the butterfly effect explained Joshua Lucas, Roberto Simmons, Travis Hunt, the carjacking outside the grocery store, and the murder outside the abandoned building. Debbie had been searching for the string tying them all together. If Ace Towing hadn't been stealing cars and placing them on the streets for "cleaning," Rainaa Mercer might still be alive. If Toni Parker hadn't flooded the streets with stolen guns, and Hank Frederich had locked his up, perhaps Travis Hunt would still be alive. The carjacking of the mom at the grocery store might never have happened.

Or would they have happened anyway?

Robertson, Parker, and Ace Towing helped fuel conditions for crime sprees, but no one had made Joshua get into the car or Roberto Simmons pull the trigger.

But at least Chase Laclede now had more to argue. Who was worse? The person who pulls the trigger or the person who puts the gun in someone's hand and encourages them to shoot?

Like Flannery, Chase had been more open with Debbie, but also spoke completely off the record. Now that Robertson was dead, and the depths of the corruption were only starting to be uncovered and would likely go deeper than many were comfortable with, he felt confident that the prosecutors might not want to push too hard against his clients.

"There's no way trying Joshua as an adult is on the table now. Judge Jamison isn't just going to let Joshua out. But he may let him go in a couple of years, provided Joshua shows he's trying to mend his ways. And with Roberto Simmons, I might be able to get a decent plea deal for him."

As for the whereabouts of the gun, and the grocery store carjackers, they were still a mystery.

These were all things Debbie knew, but couldn't write. Not yet.

But she did learn that Hawkins was the one who'd shot at her. He was the one driving the stolen car that tried to run her down. But he insisted they were just warnings, not really meant to kill her. Just scare her.

It would be up to a jury to decide whether they believed his story or not.

Even if she couldn't write about all she knew because of the off-the-record material, her stories about her ordeal went viral. The online traffic numbers set a record. And they even got hits well beyond St. Louis.

But after she'd spent a week holed up at home, padding between her room and the kitchen wearing sweatpants, her mother had declared it was enough. She was having a gathering of all the people who had reason to celebrate the dismantling of the crime ring.

Already, Debbie could hear people being let in through the front door. Debbie checked her laptop one more time.

"Debbie! Come on down," Beth called up the stairs.

The daughter dutifully shut her computer. The stories would have to wait.

The reporter descended the stairs, still a bit battered and bruised. Chase stood at the bottom of the stairs, offering his arm when she descended.

"Good to finally see you in person rather than just email and talk on the phone, Crime Beat Girl," he said teasingly.

"Ugh, please don't call me that."

The pair entered the kitchen where everyone seemed to have gathered.

"Miss Bradley!" Jarrett said, instantly embarrassed at being happy to see her.

Ada Davis set down a covered dish, then reached out to Debbie and grabbed her hand and squeezed tightly. "Oh Lord, child. What are we going to do with you? And with my grandson? You fools."

Jarrett's mom spoke. "For the record, I'm the brave one."

Sergeant Davis, who was standing nearby, shook his head.

"I hope Jarrett isn't in too much trouble," Debbie said. "I'm really sorry I got him in all this."

"Oh, he's in big trouble," Ada spoke up. "Grounded. No car. Not for a while."

But Debbie caught Jarrett smiling.

"What? That shouldn't make you happy."

"I got some good news today," he confessed.

"Yes?"

Jarrett looked at Darlinda Owens and then at Chase's mom.

Chase's mom nodded. "You can tell her. Only it's still a secret. So no stories, Debbie."

"Missouri Science and Tech got in touch with me. They think I'd make a good scholarship candidate. Depending on my ACT scores, it could be a very big one."

"That's wonderful!" Debbie said, one of many voices shouting congratulations.

Sam Hitchens, who had been standing in the living room talking with Flannery and Beth Hughes, entered. "If the kid gets a scholarship, our readers are going to love that. At least when we can print it. Our owner is going to love that. And if you write it, Crime Beat Girl, he'll love it even more."

"I think I've earned the right to demand we drop the girl. You know I hate it. Why not just stick with Crime Beat?"

"So, does that mean you're going to stay?" Sam asked.

The room fell silent, waiting for Debbie's answer. Only a knock at the door stopped Debbie before she could reply. "Who else did you invite to this?" she asked as she made her way to the door.

"I think this is it," Beth answered as Flannery stood next to the lawyer, holding a tray of food. Debbie couldn't help but notice that the detective seemed content to do her mother's bidding.

Debbie opened the door. Her heart squeezed in her chest. She hadn't prepared herself for this.

"Christian!"

"It looks like I'm interrupting something," he said, the slightly arrogant smile that Debbie always loved lighting up his face. "Are you going to invite me in?"

"Of course," Debbie said, gesturing inside.

"Everyone, I'd like you to meet…" Debbie paused, unsure how she felt about the words fiancé or even former fiancé. "Christian Garza. He's a reporter from Washington, D.C."

Christian looked at Debbie. "Well, hopefully I'm a little more than that. And I bring word from your old paper. They really want you to come back."

Debbie looked to Beth, who stood completely still. She noticed that Chase's hand seemed to tighten around his wine glass. Sam looked at the floor.

To be sure, D.C. was the capital of the country. St. Louis was yet another city on the decline. In Washington, powerful people gathered to make important decisions. St. Louis was not much more than a curious stop on old Route 66. A story about corruption in D.C. would resonate worldwide. A story about corruption in St. Louis was no different than a story about misdeed in Detroit or Chicago.

And yet, Debbie realized, *I care so much more about what happens to the people here than I ever did in D.C. Perhaps it has made a difference in my work. Maybe, just maybe, by coming home, I've become a better reporter.*

Debbie smiled, cleared her head, and raised her wine glass.

"Today, we're celebrating my story. And Jarrett's good news. And dropping *girl* from Crime Beat," Debbie announced. "The rest will have to wait."

The END

ABOUT THE AUTHOR

Geri L. Dreiling is the author of the novels "Crime Beat Girl" and "Erasing the Past."

Dreiling's background is eclectic. She is an award-winning alt-weekly journalist, a lawyer who represented clients in criminal defense matters, and she served a stint as the public information officer for the prosecutor's office in the city of St. Louis. Dreiling currently teaches media law and media ethics.

Her narrative journalism article about juvenile delinquent girls was featured in the anthology, "Notes from the Underground: The Most Outrageous Stories from the Alternative Press." She also wrote a lengthy piece, "Best Evidence," about a questionable murder conviction. Ultimately, the man won his release from prison through the efforts of The Innocence Project.

Dreiling lives in the city of St. Louis with her husband and a rescued Yorkie. Her three chickens call the backyard home. Dreiling's two children, now fully grown, have flown the coop.

Made in the USA
Monee, IL
01 July 2020

35529516R00152